SELECTED GHOST STORIES FROM KWAIDAN

SELECTED GHOST STORIES FROM KWAIDAN

LAFCADIO HEARN

EDITED BY
C. J. ANAYA

FOREWORD BY
RUSSELL DAVIS

WFP
WORDFIRE PRESS

EBook ISBN: 978-1-68057-369-5

Trade Paperback ISBN: 978-1-68057-368-8

Hardcover ISBN: 978-1-68057-370-1

Illustrations by Warm_Tail, Goyō Hashiguchi, Hokusai Onryō, Ogata Gekko, Utagawa Kuniyoshi, Sawaki Suushi, Katsukawa Shunshō, Eishi Hosoda, Utagawa Kunisada, Hiroaki Takahashi, Suzuki Kason, Ohara Koson, and Kobayashi Eitaku.

Cover design by C.J. Anaya and Allyson Longueira

Cover artwork image by Warm_Tail | Shutterstock

Published by WordFire Press, LLC

PO Box 1840 Monument CO 80132

Kevin J. Anderson & Rebecca Moesta, Publishers

WordFire Press Edition 2022

Printed in the USA

Join our WordFire Press Readers Group for new projects, and giveaways. Sign up at wordfirepress.com

CONTENTS

SOME SUSURRATIONS ABOUT THE GHOST STORY

A FOREWORD REGARDING KWAIDAN

Our fascination with the ghost story is ancient, and quite likely pre-dates any form of literature. Today, we still tell ghost stories around the campfire—often to the laughing squeals of fear and delight of young children—but it's not hard to imagine stories featuring spirits of the dead being told even before the rise of Mesopotamia (which was in 3500 BCE). No, I suspect that even when we were simple cave dwellers, torn between hunting, gathering, and hiding, the ghost story in one form or another existed.

Some believe that the earliest written form of the ghost story was Homer's *Odyssey*, which was written around the 8th or 7th century BCE, and even that is considered to have come from an oral tradition of storytelling before it was composed as a written epic. In the *Odyssey*, Odysseus journeys to the Underworld and there encounters the spirits of the dead. Other early examples include the Old Testament story of the Witch of Endor summoning the spirit of the prophet Samuel for Saul. But again, it's hard to believe that these were the first ghost stories ever written, let alone told.

The ghost story, with its focus on the spirits of the dead, is a source of endless speculation, no small amount of trepidation, and no cultural boundaries. It exists in every culture of the world and is an equal-opportunity type of tale, sparing no race, creed, or religion. We simply don't know, not for certain, what becomes of our souls upon death, and the ghost story offers a wide variety of possibilities—many of them quite disturbing. Which is a pretty good lead into Lafcadio Hearn's *Selected Stories from Kwaidan*.

First published in 1904, *Kwaidan* features several ghost stories translated by the author or told to the author who discovered them in Japan. From "The Story of Mimi-nashi Hoichi," (Hoichi the Earless, who arrived in that condition due to a ghostly samurai) a known figure from Japanese folklore to "Jikininki," literally a story about human-eating ghosts, Hearn's collection of stories is as applicable to today's reader of supernatural tales as it was when it was first published.

Hearn also includes "Yuki-onna," a story about a spirit woman that appears in the snow that he states in his introduction came to him via a farmer and has perhaps never been provided in written form, and even "Hi-Mawari," which is a recollection of one his own experiences in Wales.

The test of the ghost story for me is a difficult one. I've been reading these kinds of stories, from Poe to King to Hill to Saul and back again since I was old enough to sneak them out of the library. While many of these kinds of stories might produce an emotion likened to horror, disgust, terror, and so on, the one's that truly stay with me are the stories that produce a feeling of... disquiet. As though after I've put the book down, the author (or more likely, the narrator of the story itself) is still whispering in my ear.

I can't ever quite make these susurrations go away. They stay with me, long after I've moved on to other books or short stories. You see, a good ghost story sticks around, haunting you, much like the dead themselves.

So it is with a mix of pleasure and a bit of a warning that I'm happy to encourage you to enjoy Hearn's *Kwaidan*. I've got a feeling that at least some of these tales will stay with you, and that's why we read them.

It's okay to leave the lights on, and just ignore those sounds you might be hearing so softly in your ear. It's only your imagination, after all.

— Russell Davis
Florida, January 2022

INTRODUCTION

Most of the following Kwaidan, or Weird Tales, have been taken from old Japanese books—such as the Yaso-Kidan, Bukkyo-Hyakkwa-Zensho, Kokon-Chomonshu, Tama-Sudare, and Hyaku-Monogatari. Some of the stories may have had a Chinese origin: the very remarkable "Dream of Akinosuké," for example, is certainly from a Chinese source.

But the story-teller, in every case, has so recolored and reshaped his borrowing as to naturalize it ... One queer tale, "Yuki-Onna," was told me by a farmer of Chofu, Nishitama-gori, in Musashi province, as a legend of his native village.

Whether it has ever been written in Japanese I do not know; but the extraordinary belief which it records used certainly to exist in most parts of Japan, and in many curious forms ... The incident of "Riki-Baka" was a personal experience; and I wrote it down almost exactly as it happened, changing only a family-name mentioned by the Japanese narrator.

— L.H.
Tokyo, Japan, January 20th, 1904.

THE STORY OF MIMI-NASHI-HŌÏCHI

More than seven hundred years ago, at Dan-no-ura, in the Straits of Shimonoséki, was fought the last battle of the long contest between the Heiké, or Taira clan, and the Genji, or Minamoto clan.[1] There the Heiké perished utterly, with their women and children, and their infant emperor likewise—now remembered as Antoku Tenno.[2] And that sea and shore have been haunted for seven hundred years ... Elsewhere I told you about the strange crabs found there, called Heiké crabs, which have human faces on their backs, and are said to be the spirits of the Heiké warriors. But there are many strange things to be seen and heard along that coast. On dark nights thousands of ghostly fires hover about the beach, or flit above the waves—pale lights which the fishermen call *Oni-bi*, or demon-fires; and, whenever the winds are up, a sound of great shouting comes from that sea, like a clamor of battle.

In former years the Hecké were much more restless

1

than they now are. They would rise about ships passing in the night, and try to sink them; and at all times they would watch for swimmers, to pull them down. It was in order to appease those dead that the Buddhist temple, Amidaji, was built at Akamagaséki. A cemetery also was made close by, near the beach; and within it were set up monuments inscribed with the names of the drowned emperor and of his great vassals; and Buddhist services were regularly performed there, on behalf of the spirits of them. After the temple had been built, and the tombs erected, the Heiké gave less trouble than before; but they continued to do queer things at intervals—proving that they had not found the perfect peace.

Some centuries ago there lived at Akamagaséki a blind man named Hōïchi, who was famed for his skill in recitation and in playing upon the *biwa*.[3] From childhood he had been trained to recite and to play; and while yet a lad he had surpassed his teachers. As a professional biwa-hoshi he became famous chiefly by his recitations of the history of the Heiké and the Genji; and it is said that when he sang the song of the battle of Dan-no-ura "even the goblins [kijin] could not refrain from tears."

At the outset of his career, Hōïchi was very poor; but he found a good friend to help him. The priest of the Amidaji was fond of poetry and music; and he often invited Hōïchi to the temple, to play and recite. Afterwards, being much impressed by the wonderful skill of the lad, the priest proposed that Hōïchi should make the temple his home; and this offer was gratefully accepted. Hōïchi was given a room in the temple-building; and, in return for food and lodging, he was required only to gratify the priest with a musical performance on certain evenings, when otherwise disengaged.

One summer night the priest was called away, to perform a Buddhist service at the house of a dead parishioner; and he went there with his acolyte, leaving Hōïchi alone in the temple. It was a hot night; and the blind man sought to cool himself on the verandah before his sleeping-room. The verandah overlooked a small garden in the rear of the Amidaji. There Hōïchi waited for the priest's return, and tried to relieve his solitude by practicing upon his *biwa*. Midnight passed; and the priest did not appear. But the atmosphere was still too warm for comfort within doors; and Hōïchi remained outside. At last he heard steps approaching from the back gate. Somebody crossed the garden, advanced to the verandah, and halted directly in front of him—but it was not the priest. A deep voice called the blind man's name—abruptly and unceremoniously, in the manner of a samurai summoning an inferior:

"Hōïchi!"

Hōïchi was too much startled, for the moment, to respond; and the voice called again, in a tone of harsh command, "Hōïchi!"

"Hai!"[4] answered the blind man, frightened by the menace in the voice—"I am blind!—I cannot know who calls!"

"There is nothing to fear," the stranger exclaimed, speaking more gently. "I am stopping near this temple, and have been sent to you with a message. My present lord, a person of exceedingly high rank, is now staying in Akamagaséki, with many noble attendants. He wished to view the scene of the battle of Dan-no-ura; and to-day he visited that place. Having heard of your skill in reciting the story of the battle, he now desires to hear your performance: so you will take your *biwa* and come with me at once to the house where the august assembly is waiting."

In those times, the order of a samurai was not to be lightly disobeyed. Hōïchi donned his sandals, took his *biwa*, and went away with the stranger, who guided him deftly, but obliged him to walk very fast. The hand that guided was iron; and the clank of the warrior's stride proved him fully armed—probably some palace-guard on duty. Hōïchi's first alarm was over: he began to imagine himself in good luck; for, remembering the retainer's assurance about a "person of exceedingly high rank," he thought that the lord who wished to hear the recitation could not be less than a *daimyō* of the first class. Presently the samurai halted; and Hōïchi became aware that they had arrived at a large gateway;—and he wondered, for he could not remember any large gate in that part of the town, except the main gate of the Amidaji.

"Kaimon!"[5] the samurai called—and there was a sound of unbarring; and the twain passed on. They traversed a space of garden, and halted again before some entrance; and the retainer cried in a loud voice, "Within there! I have brought Hōïchi."

Then came sounds of feet hurrying, and screens sliding, and rain-doors opening, and voices of women in converse. By the language of the women Hōïchi knew them to be domestics in some noble household; but he could not imagine to what place he had been conducted. Little time was allowed him for conjecture. After he had been helped to mount several stone steps, upon the last of which he was told to leave his sandals, a woman's hand guided him along interminable reaches of polished planking, and round pillared angles too many to remember, and over widths amazing of matted floor—into the middle of some vast apartment. There he thought that many great people were assembled: the sound of the rustling of silk was like the sound of leaves in a forest. He heard also a great humming of voices—talking in undertones; and the speech was the speech of courts.

Hōïchi was told to put himself at ease, and he found a kneeling-cushion ready for him. After having taken his place upon it, and tuned his instrument, the voice of a woman—whom he divined to be the *Rōjo*, or matron in charge of the female service—addressed him, saying, "It is now required that the history of the Heiké be recited, to the accompaniment of the biwa."

Now the entire recital would have required a time of many nights: therefore Hōïchi ventured a question:

"As the whole of the story is not soon told, what portion is it augustly desired that I now recite?"

The woman's voice made answer:

"Recite the story of the battle at Dan-no-ura—for the pity of it is the most deep."[6]

Then Hōïchi lifted up his voice, and chanted the chant of the fight on the bitter sea—wonderfully making his *biwa* to sound like the straining of oars and the rushing of ships, the whirr and the hissing of arrows, the shouting and trampling of men, the crashing of steel upon helmets, the plunging of slain in the flood. And to left and right of him, in the pauses of his playing, he could hear voices murmuring praise: "How marvelous an artist!"—"Never in our own province was playing heard like this!"—"Not in all the empire is there another singer like Hōïchi!"

Then fresh courage came to him, and he played and sang yet better than before; and a hush of wonder deepened about him. But when at last he came to tell the fate of the fair and helpless—the piteous perishing of the women and children—and the death-leap of Nii-no-Ama, with the imperial infant in her arms—then all the listeners uttered together one long, long shuddering cry of anguish; and thereafter they wept and wailed so loudly and so wildly that the blind man was frightened by the violence and grief that he had made. For much time the sobbing and the wailing continued. But gradually the sounds of lamentation died away; and again, in the great stillness that followed, Hōïchi heard the voice of the woman whom he supposed to be the *Rōjo*.

She said:

"Although we had been assured that you were a very skillful player upon the *biwa*, and without an equal in recitative, we did not know that anyone could be so skillful as you have proved yourself to-night. Our lord has been pleased to say that he intends to bestow upon you a fitting reward. But he desires that you shall perform before him once every night for the next six nights—after which time he will probably make his august return-journey. To-morrow night, therefore, you are to come here at the same hour. The retainer who to-night conducted you will be sent for you ... There is another matter about which I have been ordered to inform you. It is required that you shall speak to no one of your visits here, during the time of our lord's august sojourn at Akamagaséki. As he is traveling incognito,[7] he commands that no mention of these things be made ... You are now free to go back to your temple."

After Hōïchi had duly expressed his thanks, a woman's hand conducted him to the entrance of the house, where the same retainer, who had before guided him, was waiting to take him home. The retainer led him to the verandah at the rear of the temple, and there bade him farewell.

It was almost dawn when Hōïchi returned; but his absence from the temple had not been observed—as the priest, coming back at a very late hour, had supposed him asleep. During the day Hōïchi was able to take some rest; and he said nothing about his strange adventure. In the middle of the following night the samurai again came for him, and led him to the august assembly, where he gave another recitation with the same success that had attended his previous performance. But during this second visit his absence from the temple was accidentally discovered; and after his return in the morning he was summoned to the presence of the priest, who said to him, in a tone of kindly reproach:

"We have been very anxious about you, friend Hōïchi. To go out, blind and alone, at so late an hour, is danger-ous. Why did you go without telling us? I could have ordered a servant to accompany you. And where have you been?"

Hōïchi answered, evasively, "Pardon me kind friend! I had to attend to some private business; and I could not arrange the matter at any other hour."

The priest was surprised, rather than pained, by

Hōïchi's reticence: he felt it to be unnatural, and suspected something wrong. He feared that the blind lad had been bewitched or deluded by some evil spirits. He did not ask any more questions; but he privately instructed the men-servants of the temple to keep watch upon Hōïchi's movements, and to follow him in case that he should again leave the temple after dark.

On the very next night, Hōïchi was seen to leave the temple; and the servants immediately lighted their lanterns, and followed after him. But it was a rainy night, and very dark; and before the temple-folks could get to the roadway, Hōïchi had disappeared. Evidently he had walked very fast—a strange thing, considering his blindness; for the road was in a bad condition. The men hurried through the streets, making inquiries at every house which Hōïchi was accustomed to visit; but nobody could give them any news of him. At last, as they were returning to the temple by way of the shore, they were startled by the sound of a *biwa*, furiously played, in the cemetery of the Amidaji. Except for some ghostly fires—such as usually flitted there on dark nights—all was blackness in that direction. But the men at once hastened to the cemetery; and there, by the help of their lanterns, they discovered Hōïchi—sitting alone in the rain before the memorial tomb of Antoku Tenno, making his *biwa* resound, and loudly chanting the chant of the battle of Dan-no-ura. And behind him, and about him, and everywhere above the tombs, the fires of the dead were burning, like candles. Never before had so great a host of *Oni-bi* appeared in the sight of mortal man.

"Hōïchi San!—Hōïchi San!" the servants cried—"you are bewitched! ... Hōïchi San!"

But the blind man did not seem to hear. Strenuously he made his *biwa* to rattle and ring and clang—more and more wildly he chanted the chant of the battle of Dan-no-ura. They caught hold of him—they shouted into his ear, "Hōïchi San!—Hōïchi San!—come home with us at once!"

Reprovingly he spoke to them:

"To interrupt me in such a manner, before this august assembly, will not be tolerated."

Whereat, in spite of the weirdness of the thing, the servants could not help laughing. Sure that he had been bewitched, they now seized him, and pulled him up on his feet, and by main force hurried him back to the temple —where he was immediately relieved of his wet clothes, by order of the priest. Then the priest insisted upon a full explanation of his friend's astonishing behavior.

Hōïchi long hesitated to speak. But at last, finding that his conduct had really alarmed and angered the good priest, he decided to abandon his reserve; and he related everything that had happened from the time of first visit of the samurai.

The priest said:

"Hōïchi, my poor friend, you are now in great danger! How unfortunate that you did not tell me all this before! Your wonderful skill in music has indeed brought you into strange trouble. By this time you must be aware that you have not been visiting any house whatever, but have been passing your nights in the cemetery, among the tombs of the Heiké—and it was before the memorial-tomb of Antoku Tennō that our people to-night found you, sitting

9

in the rain. All that you have been imagining was illusion —except the calling of the dead. By once obeying them, you have put yourself in their power. If you obey them again, after what has already occurred, they will tear you in pieces. But they would have destroyed you, sooner or later, in any event ... Now I shall not be able to remain with you to-night: I am called away to perform another service. But, before I go, it will be necessary to protect your body by writing holy texts upon it."

Before sundown the priest and his acolyte stripped Hōïchi: then, with their writing-brushes, they traced upon his breast and back, head and face and neck, limbs and hands and feet—even upon the soles of his feet, and upon all parts of his body—the text of the holy sûtra called *Hannya-Shin-Kyo*.[8] When this had been done, the priest instructed Hōïchi, saying:

"To-night, as soon as I go away, you must seat yourself on the verandah, and wait. You will be called. But, whatever may happen, do not answer, and do not move. Say nothing and sit still—as if meditating. If you stir, or make any noise, you will be torn asunder. Do not get frightened; and do not think of calling for help—because no help could save you. If you do exactly as I tell you, the danger will pass, and you will have nothing more to fear."

After dark the priest and the acolyte went away; and Hōïchi seated himself on the verandah, according to the instructions given him. He laid his *biwa* on the planking beside him, and, assuming the attitude of meditation, remained quite still—taking care not to cough, or to breathe audibly. For hours he stayed thus.

Then, from the roadway, he heard the steps coming.

They passed the gate, crossed the garden, approached the verandah, stopped—directly in front of him.

"Hōïchi!" the deep voice called. But the blind man held his breath, and sat motionless. "Hōïchi!" grimly called the voice a second time. Then a third time —savagely:

"Hōïchi!"

Hōïchi remained as still as a stone—and the voice grumbled:

"No answer!—that won't do! ... Must see where the fellow is."

There was a noise of heavy feet mounting upon the verandah. The feet approached deliberately—halted beside him. Then, for long minutes—during which Hōïchi felt his whole body shake to the beating of his heart— there was dead silence.

At last the gruff voice muttered close to him:

"Here is the *biwa*; but of the biwa-player I see—only two ears! ... So that explains why he did not answer: he had no mouth to answer with—there is nothing left of

him but his ears ... Now to my lord those ears I will take—
in proof that the august commands have been obeyed, so
far as was possible."

At that instant Hōïchi felt his ears gripped by fingers
of iron, and torn off! Great as the pain was, he gave no cry.
The heavy footfalls receded along the verandah—
descended into the garden—passed out to the roadway—
ceased. From either side of his head, the blind man felt a
thick warm trickling; but he dared not lift his hands.

Before sunrise the priest came back. He hastened at
once to the verandah in the rear, stepped and slipped
upon something clammy, and uttered a cry of horror—for
he saw, by the light of his lantern, that the clamminess
was blood. But he perceived Hōïchi sitting there, in the
attitude of meditation—with the blood still oozing from
his wounds.

"My poor Hōïchi!" cried the startled priest—"what is
this? ... You have been hurt?"

At the sound of his friend's voice, the blind man felt
safe. He burst out sobbing, and tearfully told his adventure of the night.

"Poor, poor Hōïchi!" the priest exclaimed—"all my
fault!—my very grievous fault! ... Everywhere upon your
body the holy texts had been written—except upon your
ears! I trusted my acolyte to do that part of the work; and
it was very, very wrong of me not to have made sure that
he had done it! ... Well, the matter cannot now be helped:
we can only try to heal your hurts as soon as possible ...
Cheer up, friend!—the danger is now well over. You will
never again be troubled by those visitors."

With the aid of a good doctor, Hōïchi soon recovered

from his injuries. The story of his strange adventure spread far and wide, and soon made him famous. Many noble persons went to Akamagaséki to hear him recite; and large presents of money were given to him—so that he became a wealthy man ... But from the time of his adventure, he was known only by the appellation of *Mimi-nashi-Hōïchi*: "Hōïchi-the-Earless."

OSHIDORI

There was a falconer and hunter, named Sonjo, who lived in the district called Tamura-no-Go, of the province of Mutsu. One day he went out hunting, and could not find any game. But on his way home, at a place called Akanuma, he perceived a pair of oshidori[1] (mandarin-ducks), swimming together in a river that he was about to cross. To kill oshidori is not good; but Sonjo happened to be very hungry, and he shot at the pair. His arrow pierced the male: the female escaped into the rushes of the further shore, and disappeared. Sonjo took the dead bird home, and cooked it.

That night he dreamed a dreary dream. It seemed to him that a beautiful woman came into his room, and stood by his pillow, and began to weep. So bitterly did she weep that Sonjo felt as if his heart were being torn out while he listened.

And the woman cried to him:

"Why—oh! Why did you kill him?—of what wrong was he guilty? ... At Akanuma we were so happy to-gether —and you killed him! ... What harm did he ever do you? Do you even know what you have done?—oh! Do you

know what a cruel, what a wicked thing you have done? ...
Me too you have killed,—for I will not live without my
husband! ... Only to tell you this I came."

Then again she wept aloud—so bitterly that the voice
of her crying pierced into the marrow of the listener's
bones;—and she sobbed out the words of this poem:

> *Hi kururéba*
> *Sasoeshi mono wo—*
> *Akanuma no*
> *Makomo no kure no*
> *Hitori-né zo uki!*

["At the coming of twilight I invited him to return
with me—! Now to sleep alone in the shadow of the
rushes of Akanuma—ah! What misery unspeakable!"][2]

And after having uttered these verses she exclaimed:

"Ah, you do not know—you cannot know what you
have done! But to-morrow, when you go to Akanuma, you
will see—you will see...." So saying, and weeping very
piteously, she went away.

When Sonjo awoke in the morning, this dream
remained so vivid in his mind that he was greatly troubled. He remembered the words:

"But to-morrow, when you go to Akanuma, you will
see—you will see."

And he resolved to go there at once, that he might
learn whether his dream was anything more than a
dream. So he went to Akanuma; and there, when he came
to the riverbank, he saw the female oshidori swimming
alone.

In the same moment the bird perceived Sonjo; but, instead of trying to escape, she swam straight towards him, looking at him the while in a strange-fixed way. Then, with her beak, she suddenly tore open her own body, and died before the hunter's eyes ... Sonjo shaved his head and became a priest.

THE STORY OF O-TEI

A long time ago, in the town of Niigata, in the province of Echizen, there lived a man called Nagao Chosei. Nagao was the son of a physician, and was educated for his father's profession. At an early age he had been betrothed to a girl called O-Tei, the daughter of one of his father's friends; and both families had agreed that the wedding should take place as soon as Nagao had finished his studies. But the health of O-Tei proved to be weak; and in her fifteenth year she was attacked by a fatal consumption. When she became aware that she must die, she sent for Nagao to bid him farewell.

As he knelt at her bedside, she said to him:

"Nagao-Sama,[1] my betrothed, we were promised to each other from the time of our childhood; and we were to have been married at the end of this year. But now I am going to die;—the gods know what is best for us. If I were able to live for some years longer, I could only continue to be a cause of trouble and grief for others. With this frail body, I could not be a good wife; and therefore even to wish to live, for your sake, would be a very selfish wish. I am quite resigned to die; and I want you to promise that you will not grieve ... Besides, I want to tell you that I think we shall meet again."

"Indeed we shall meet again," Nagao answered earnestly. "And in that Pure Land[2] there will be no pain of separation."

"Nay, nay!" she responded softly, "I meant not the Pure Land. I believe that we are destined to meet again in this world—although I shall be buried to-morrow."

Nagao looked at her wonderingly, and saw her smile at his wonder. She continued, in her gentle, dreamy voice:

"Yes, I mean in this world—in your own present life, Nagao-Sama ... Providing, indeed, that you wish it. Only, for this thing to happen, I must again be born a girl, and grow up to womanhood. So you would have to wait. Fifteen—sixteen years: that is a long time ... But, my promised husband, you are now only nineteen years old."

Eager to soothe her dying moments, he answered tenderly:

"To wait for you, my betrothed, were no less a joy than a duty. We are pledged to each other for the time of seven existences."

"But you doubt?" she questioned, watching his face.

"My dear one," he answered, "I doubt whether I should be able to know you in another body, under another name—unless you can tell me of a sign or token."

"That I cannot do," she said. "Only the Gods and the Buddhas know how and where we shall meet. But I am sure—very, very sure—that, if you be not unwilling to receive me, I shall be able to come back to you ... Remember these words of mine."

She ceased to speak; and her eyes closed. She was dead.

Nagao had been sincerely attached to O-Tei; and his grief was deep. He had a mortuary tablet made, inscribed with her zokumyo;[3] and he placed the tablet in his *butsudan*,[4] and every day set offerings before it. He thought a great deal about the strange things that O-Tei had said to him just before her death; and, in the hope of pleasing her spirit, he wrote a solemn promise to wed her if she could ever return to him in another body. This written promise he sealed with his seal, and placed in the butsudan beside the mortuary tablet of O-Tei.

Nevertheless, as Nagao was an only son, it was necessary that he should marry. He soon found himself obliged to yield to the wishes of his family, and to accept a wife of his father's choosing. After his marriage he continued to set offerings before the tablet of O-Tei; and he never failed to remember her with affection. But by degrees her image became dim in his memory—like a dream that is hard to recall.

And the years went by.

During those years many misfortunes came upon him. He lost his parents by death—then his wife and his only child. So that he found himself alone in the world. He abandoned his desolate home, and set out upon a long journey in the hope of forgetting his sorrows.

One day, in the course of his travels, he arrived at Ikao —a mountain-village still famed for its thermal springs, and for the beautiful scenery of its neighborhood. In the village-inn at which he stopped, a young girl came to wait upon him; and, at the first sight of her face, he felt his heart leap as it had never leaped before.

So strangely did she resemble O-Tei that he pinched himself to make sure that he was not dreaming. As she went and came—bringing fire and food, or arranging the chamber of the guest—her every attitude and motion revived in him some gracious memory of the girl to whom he had been pledged in his youth.

He spoke to her; and she responded in a soft, clear voice of which the sweetness saddened him with a sadness of other days.

Then, in great wonder, he questioned her, saying:

"Elder Sister,[5] so much do you look like a person whom I knew long ago, that I was startled when you first entered this room. Pardon me, therefore, for asking what is your native place, and what is your name?"

Immediately—and in the unforgotten voice of the dead—she thus made answer:

"My name is O-Tei; and you are Nagao Chosei of Echigo, my promised husband. Seventeen years ago, I died in Niigata: then you made in writing a promise to marry me if ever I could come back to this world in the body of a woman;—and you sealed that written promise with your seal, and put it in the *butsudan*, beside the tablet inscribed with my name. And therefore I came back."

As she uttered these last words, she fell unconscious.

Nagao married her; and the marriage was a happy one. But at no time afterwards could she remember what she had told him in answer to his question at Ikao: neither could she remember anything of her previous existence.

The recollection of the former birth—mysteriously kindled in the moment of that meeting—had again become obscured, and so thereafter remained.

UBAZAKURA

Three hundred years ago, in the village called Asamimura, in the district called Onsengori, in the province of Iyo, there lived a good man named Tokubei. This Tokubei was the richest person in the district, and the muraosa, or headman, of the village. In most matters he was fortunate; but he reached the age of forty without knowing the happiness of becoming a father. Therefore he and his wife, in the affliction of their childlessness, addressed many prayers to the divinity Fudo Myo O, who had a famous temple, called Saihoji, in Asamimura.

At last their prayers were heard: the wife of Tokubei gave birth to a daughter. The child was very pretty; and she received the name of Tsuyu. As the mother's milk was deficient, a milk-nurse, called O-Sode, was hired for the little one.

O-Tsuyu grew up to be a very beautiful girl; but at the age of fifteen she fell sick, and the doctors thought that she was going to die. In that time the nurse O-Sode, who loved O-Tsuyu with a real mother's love, went to the temple Saihoji, and fervently prayed to Fudo-Sama on behalf of the girl.

Every day, for twenty-one days, she went to the temple and prayed; and at the end of that time, O-Tsuyu suddenly and completely recovered.

Then there was great rejoicing in the house of Tokubei; and he gave a feast to all his friends in celebration of the happy event. But on the night of the feast the nurse O-Sode was suddenly taken ill; and on the following morning, the doctor, who had been summoned to attend her, announced that she was dying.

Then the family, in great sorrow, gathered about her bed, to bid her farewell.

But she said to them:

"It is time that I should tell you something which you do not know. My prayer has been heard. I besought Fudo-Sama that I might be permitted to die in the place of O-Tsuyu; and this great favor has been granted me. Therefore you must not grieve about my death ... But I have one request to make. I promised Fudo-Sama that I would have a cherry-tree planted in the garden of Saihoji, for a thank-offering and a commemoration. Now I shall not be able myself to plant the tree there: so I must beg that you will fulfill that vow for me ... Good-bye, dear friends; and remember that I was happy to die for O-Tsuyu's sake."

After the funeral of O-Sode, a young cherry-tree—the finest that could be found—was planted in the garden of Saihoji by the parents of O-Tsuyu.

The tree grew and flourished; and on the sixteenth day of the second month of the following year—the anniversary of O-Sode's death—it blossomed in a wonderful way.

So it continued to blossom for two hundred and fifty-four years—always upon the sixteenth day of the second month;—and its flowers, pink and white, were like the nipples of a woman's breasts, bedewed with milk. And the people called it Ubazakura, the Cherry-tree of the Milk-Nurse.

DIPLOMACY

It had been ordered that the execution should take place in the garden of the yashiki.[1] So the man was taken there, and made to kneel down in a wide sanded space crossed by a line of tobi-ishi, or stepping-stones, such as you may still see in Japanese landscape-gardens. His arms were bound behind him. Retainers brought water in buckets, and rice-bags filled with pebbles; and they packed the rice-bags round the kneeling man—so wedging him in that he could not move. The master came, and observed the arrangements. He found them satisfactory, and made no remarks.

Suddenly the condemned man cried out to him:

"Honored Sir, the fault for which I have been doomed I did not wittingly commit. It was only my very great stupidity which caused the fault. Having been born stupid, by reason of my Karma, I could not always help making mistakes. But to kill a man for being stupid is wrong—and that wrong will be repaid. So surely as you kill me, so surely shall I be avenged—out of the resentment that you provoke will come the vengeance; and evil will be rendered for evil."

If any person be killed while feeling strong resentment, the ghost of that person will be able to take vengeance upon the killer. This the samurai knew. He replied very gently—almost caressingly:

"We shall allow you to frighten us as much as you please—after you are dead. But it is difficult to believe that you mean what you say. Will you try to give us some sign of your great resentment—after your head has been cut off?"

"Assuredly I will," answered the man.

"Very well," said the samurai, drawing his long sword —"I am now going to cut off your head. Directly in front of you there is a stepping-stone. After your head has been cut off, try to bite the stepping-stone. If your angry ghost can help you to do that, some of us may be frightened ... Will you try to bite the stone?"

"I will bite it!" cried the man, in great anger—"I will bite it!—I will bite"—

There was a flash, a swish, a crunching thud: the bound body bowed over the rice sacks—two long blood-jets pumping from the shorn neck—and the head rolled upon the sand. Heavily toward the stepping-stone it rolled: then, suddenly bounding, it caught the upper edge of the stone between its teeth, clung desperately for a moment, and dropped inert.

None spoke; but the retainers stared in horror at their master. He seemed to be quite unconcerned.

He merely held out his sword to the nearest atten-
dant, who, with a wooden dipper, poured water over the
blade from haft to point, and then carefully wiped the
steel several times with sheets of soft paper ... And thus
ended the ceremonial part of the incident.

For months thereafter, the retainers and the domestics lived in ceaseless fear of ghostly visitation. None of
them doubted that the promised vengeance would come;
and their constant terror caused them to hear and to see
much that did not exist. They became afraid of the sound
of the wind in the bamboos—afraid even of the stirring of
shadows in the garden. At last, after taking counsel
together, they decided to petition their master to have a
Segaki-service[2] performed on behalf of the vengeful
spirit.

"Quite unnecessary," the samurai said, when his chief
retainer had uttered the general wish ... "I understand

that the desire of a dying man for revenge may be a cause for fear. But in this case there is nothing to fear."

The retainer looked at his master beseechingly, but hesitated to ask the reason of the alarming confidence.

"Oh, the reason is simple enough," declared the samurai, divining the unspoken doubt. "Only the very last intention of the fellow could have been dangerous; and when I challenged him to give me the sign, I diverted his mind from the desire of revenge. He died with the set purpose of biting the stepping-stone; and that purpose he was able to accomplish, but nothing else. All the rest he must have forgotten ... So you need not feel any further anxiety about the matter."

And indeed the dead man gave no more trouble. Nothing at all happened.

OF A MIRROR
AND A BELL

E ight centuries ago, the priests of Mugenyama, in
the province of Totomi,[1] wanted a big bell for
their temple; and they asked the women of their
parish to help them by contributing old bronze mirrors
for bell-metal.

[Even to-day, in the courts of certain Japanese
temples, you may see heaps of old bronze mirrors
contributed for such a purpose. The largest collection of
this kind that I ever saw was in the court of a temple of
the Jodo sect, at Hakata, in Kyushu: the mirrors had been
given for the making of a bronze statue of Amida, thirty-
three feet high.]

There was at that time a young woman, a farmer's
wife, living at Mugenyama, who presented her mirror to
the temple, to be used for bell-metal. But afterwards she
much regretted her mirror. She remembered things that
her mother had told her about it; and she remembered
that it had belonged, not only to her mother but to her

mother's mother and grandmother; and she remembered some happy smiles which it had reflected. Of course, if she could have offered the priests a certain sum of money in place of the mirror, she could have asked them to give back her heirloom. But she had not the money necessary.

Whenever she went to the temple, she saw her mirror lying in the courtyard, behind a railing, among hundreds of other mirrors heaped there together. She knew it by the Sho-Chiku-Bai in relief on the back of it—those three fortunate emblems of Pine, Bamboo, and Plum flower, which delighted her baby-eyes when her mother first showed her the mirror. She longed for some chance to steal the mirror, and hide it—that she might thereafter treasure it always. But the chance did not come; and she became very unhappy—felt as if she had foolishly given away a part of her life. She thought about the old saying that a mirror is the Soul of a Woman—(a saying mystically expressed, by the Chinese character for Soul, upon the backs of many bronze mirrors)—and she feared that it was true in weirder ways than she had before imagined. But she could not dare to speak of her pain to anybody.

Now, when all the mirrors contributed for the Mugenyama bell had been sent to the foundry, the bell-founders discovered that there was one mirror among them which would not melt. Again and again they tried to melt it; but it resisted all their efforts. Evidently the woman who had given that mirror to the temple must have regretted the giving. She had not presented her offering with all her heart; and therefore her selfish soul, remaining attached to the mirror, kept it hard and cold in the midst of the furnace.

Of course everybody heard of the matter, and everybody soon knew whose mirror it was that would not melt. And because of this public exposure of her secret fault, the poor woman became very much ashamed and very angry. And as she could not bear the shame, she drowned herself, after having written a farewell letter containing these words:

"When I am dead, it will not be difficult to melt the mirror and to cast the bell. But, to the person who breaks that bell by ringing it, great wealth will be given by the ghost of me." You must know that the last wish or promise of anybody who dies in anger, or performs suicide in anger, is generally supposed to possess a supernatural force. After the dead woman's mirror had been melted, and the bell had been successfully cast, people remembered the words of that letter. They felt sure that the spirit of the writer would give wealth to the breaker of the bell; and, as soon as the bell had been suspended in the court of the temple, they went in multitude to ring it.

With all their might and main they swung the ringing-beam; but the bell proved to be a good bell, and it bravely withstood their assaults. Nevertheless, the people were not easily discouraged. Day after day, at all hours, they continued to ring the bell furiously—caring nothing whatever for the protests of the priests. So the ringing became an affliction; and the priests could not endure it; and they got rid of the bell by rolling it down the hill into a swamp. The swamp was deep, and swallowed it up—and that was the end of the bell. Only its legend remains; and in that legend it is called the Mugen-Kane, or Bell of Mugen.

Now there are queer old Japanese beliefs in the magical efficacy of a certain mental operation implied, though not described, by the verb nazoraeru. The word itself cannot be adequately rendered by any English word;

for it is used in relation to many kinds of mimetic magic, as well as in relation to the performance of many religious acts of faith.

Common meanings of nazoraeru, according to dictionaries, are "to imitate," "to compare," "to liken;" but the esoteric meaning is to substitute, in imagination, one object or action for another, so as to bring about some magical or miraculous result.

For example: you cannot afford to build a Buddhist temple; but you can easily lay a pebble before the image of the Buddha, with the same pious feeling that would prompt you to build a temple if you were rich enough to build one.

The merit of so offering the pebble becomes equal, or almost equal, to the merit of erecting a temple ... You cannot read the six thousand seven hundred and seventy-one volumes of the Buddhist texts; but you can make a revolving library, containing them, turn round, by pushing it like a windlass.

And if you push with an earnest wish that you could read the six thousand seven hundred and seventy-one volumes, you will acquire the same merit as the reading of them would enable you to gain ... So much will perhaps suffice to explain the religious meanings of nazoraeru.

The magical meanings could not all be explained without a great variety of examples; but, for present purposes, the following will serve. If you should make a little man of straw, for the same reason that Sister Helen made a little man of wax—and nail it, with nails not less than five inches long, to some tree in a temple-grove at the Hour of the Ox[2]—and if the person, imaginatively represented by that little straw man, should die thereafter in atrocious agony —that would illustrate one signification of nazo-raeru ... Or, let us suppose that a robber has entered your house during the night, and carried away your valuables.

If you can discover the footprints of that robber in your garden, and then promptly burn a very large moxa on each of them, the soles of the feet of the robber will become inflamed, and will allow him no rest until he returns, of his own accord, to put himself at your mercy. That is another kind of mimetic magic expressed by the term nazoraeru. And a third kind is illustrated by various legends of the Mugen-Kane.

After the bell had been rolled into the swamp, there was, of course, no more chance of ringing it in such wise as to break it. But persons who regretted this loss of opportunity would strike and break objects imaginatively substituted for the bell—thus hoping to please the spirit of the owner of the mirror that had made so much trouble. One of these persons was a woman called Umegae—famed in Japanese legend because of her relation to Kaji-wara Kagesue, a warrior of the Heiké clan.

While the pair were traveling together, Kajiwara one day found himself in great straits for want of money; and Umegae, remembering the tradition of the Bell of Mugen, took a basin of bronze, and, mentally representing it to be the bell, beat upon it until she broke it—crying out, at the same time, for three hundred pieces of gold. A guest of the inn where the pair were stopping made inquiry as to the cause of the banging and the crying, and, on learning the story of the trouble, actually presented Umegae with three hundred ryo[3] in gold.

Afterwards a song was made about Umegae's basin of bronze; and that song is sung by dancing girls even to this day:

> *Umegae no chozubachi tataite*
> *O-kane ga deru naraba*
> *Mina San mi-uke wo*
> *Sore tanomimasu*

["If, by striking upon the wash-basin of Umegae, I could make honorable money come to me, then would I negotiate for the freedom of all my girl-comrades."]

After this happening, the fame of the Mugen-Kane became great; and many people followed the example of Umegae—thereby hoping to emulate her luck. Among these folk was a dissolute farmer who lived near Mugenyama, on the bank of the Oigawa.

Having wasted his substance in riotous living, this farmer made for himself, out of the mud in his garden, a clay-model of the Mugen-Kane; and he beat the clay-bell, and broke it—crying out the while for great wealth.

Then, out of the ground before him, rose up the figure of a white-robed woman, with long loose-flowing hair, holding a covered jar.

And the woman said:

"I have come to answer your fervent prayer as it deserves to be answered. Take, therefore, this jar." So saying, she put the jar into his hands, and disappeared.

Into his house the happy man rushed, to tell his wife

the good news. He set down in front of her the covered jar
—which was heavy—and they opened it together. And
they found that it was filled, up to the very brim, with.

But no!—I really cannot tell you with what it was
filled.

JIKININKI

Once, when Musō Kokushi, a priest of the Zen sect, was journeying alone through the province of Mino,[1] he lost his way in a mountain-district where there was nobody to direct him. For a long time he wandered about helplessly; and he was beginning to despair of finding shelter for the night, when he perceived, on the top of a hill lighted by the last rays of the sun, one of those little hermitages, called *anjitsu*, which are built for solitary priests. It seemed to be in ruinous condition; but he hastened to it eagerly, and found that it was inhabited by an aged priest, from whom he begged the favor of a night's lodging. This the old man harshly refused; but he directed Musō to a certain hamlet, in the valley adjoining where lodging and food could be obtained.

Musō found his way to the hamlet, which consisted of less than a dozen farm-cottages; and he was kindly received at the dwelling of the headman. Forty or fifty persons were assembled in the principal apartment, at the moment of Musō's arrival; but he was shown into a small separate room, where he was promptly supplied with food and bedding. Being very tired, he lay down to rest at an early hour; but a little before midnight he was roused from sleep by a sound of loud weeping in the next apartment. Presently the sliding-screens were gently pushed apart; and a young man, carrying a lighted lantern, entered the room, respectfully saluted him, and said:

"Reverend Sir, it is my painful duty to tell you that I am now the responsible head of this house. Yesterday I was only the eldest son. But when you came here, tired as you were, we did not wish that you should feel embarrassed in any way: therefore we did not tell you that father had died only a few hours before. The people whom you saw in the next room are the inhabitants of this village: they all assembled here to pay their last respects to the dead; and now they are going to another village, about three miles off—for by our custom, no one of us may remain in this village during the night after a death has taken place. We make the proper offerings and prayers; then we go away, leaving the corpse alone. Strange things always happen in the house where a corpse has thus been left: so we think that it will be better for you to come away with us. We can find you good lodging in the other village. But perhaps, as you are a priest, you have no fear of demons or evil spirits; and, if you are not afraid of being left alone with the body, you will be very welcome to the use of this poor house.

However, I must tell you that nobody, except a priest, would dare to remain here tonight."

Musō made answer:

"For your kind intention and your generous hospitality, I am deeply grateful. But I am sorry that you did not tell me of your father's death when I came; for, though I was a little tired, I certainly was not so tired that I should have found difficulty in doing my duty as a priest. Had you told me, I could have performed the service before your departure. As it is, I shall perform the service after you have gone away; and I shall stay by the body until morning. I do not know what you mean by your words about the danger of staying here alone; but I am not afraid of ghosts or demons: therefore please to feel no anxiety on my account."

The young man appeared to be rejoiced by these assurances, and expressed his gratitude in fitting words. Then the other members of the family, and the folk assembled in the adjoining room, having been told of the priest's kind promises, came to thank him—after which the master of the house said:

"Now, reverend Sir, much as we regret to leave you alone, we must bid you farewell. By the rule of our village, none of us can stay here after midnight. We beg, kind Sir, that you will take every care of your honorable body, while we are unable to attend upon you. And if you happen to hear or see anything strange during our absence, please tell us of the matter when we return in the morning."

All then left the house, except the priest, who went to the

room where the dead body was lying. The usual offerings had been set before the corpse; and a small Buddhist lamp —*tomyo*—was burning. The priest recited the service, and performed the funeral ceremonies—after which he entered into meditation. So meditating he remained through several silent hours; and there was no sound in the deserted village. But, when the hush of the night was at its deepest, there noiselessly entered a Shape, vague and vast; and in the same moment Musō found himself without power to move or speak. He saw that Shape lift the corpse, as with hands, devour it, more quickly than a cat devours a rat—beginning at the head, and eating everything: the hair and the bones and even the shroud. And the monstrous Thing, having thus consumed the body, turned to the offerings, and ate them also. Then it went away, as mysteriously as it had come.

When the villagers returned next morning, they found the priest awaiting them at the door of the head-man's dwelling. All in turn saluted him; and when they had entered, and looked about the room, no one expressed any surprise at the disappearance of the dead body and the offerings. But the master of the house said to Musō:

"Reverent Sir, you have probably seen unpleasant things during the night: all of us were anxious about you. But now we are very happy to find you alive and unharmed. Gladly we would have stayed with you, if it had been possible. But the law of our village, as I told you last evening, obliges us to quit our houses after a death has taken place, and to leave the corpse alone. Whenever this law has been broken, heretofore, some great misfortune has followed. Whenever it is obeyed, we find that the corpse and the offerings disappear during our absence. Perhaps you have seen the cause."

Then Musō told of the dim and awful Shape that had entered the death-chamber to devour the body and the offerings.

No person seemed to be surprised by his narration; and the master of the house observed:

"What you have told us, reverend Sir, agrees with what has been said about this matter from ancient time."

Musō then inquired:

"Does not the priest on the hill sometimes perform the funeral service for your dead?"

"What priest?" the young man asked.

"The priest who yesterday evening directed me to this village," answered Musō. "I called at his *anjitsu* on the hill yonder. He refused me lodging, but told me the way here."

The listeners looked at each other, as in astonishment; and, after a moment of silence, the master of the house said:

"Reverend Sir, there is no priest and there is no *anjitsu* on the hill. For the time of many generations there has not been any resident-priest in this neighborhood."

Musō said nothing more on the subject; for it was evident that his kind hosts supposed him to have been deluded by some goblin. But after having bidden them farewell, and obtained all necessary information as to his road, he determined to look again for the hermitage on the hill, and so to ascertain whether he had really been deceived. He found the *anjitsu* without any difficulty; and, this time, its aged occupant invited him to enter. When he had done so, the hermit humbly bowed down before him, exclaiming:

"Ah! I am ashamed!—I am very much ashamed!—I am exceedingly ashamed!"

"You need not be ashamed for having refused me shelter," said Musō. "You directed me to the village yonder, where I was very kindly treated; and I thank you for that favor."

"I can give no man shelter," the recluse made answer; and it is not for the refusal that I am ashamed. I am ashamed only that you should have seen me in my real shape—for it was I who devoured the corpse and the offerings last night before your eyes ... Know, reverend Sir, that I am a jikininki,[2]—an eater of human flesh. Have pity upon me, and suffer me to confess the secret fault by which I became reduced to this condition.

"A long, long time ago, I was a priest in this desolate region. There was no other priest for many leagues around. So, in that time, the bodies of the mountain-folk who died used to be brought here—sometimes from great distances—in order that I might repeat over them the holy service. But I repeated the service and performed the rites only as a matter of business; I thought only of the food and the clothes that my sacred profession enabled me to gain. And because of this selfish impiety I was reborn, immediately after my death, into the state of a *jikininki.* Since then I have been obliged to feed upon the corpses of the people who die in this district: every one of them I must devour in the way that you saw last night ... Now, reverend Sir, let me beseech you to perform a *Ségaki*-service[3] for me: help me by your prayers, I entreat you, so that I may be soon able to escape from this horrible state of existence."

No sooner had the hermit uttered this petition than he disappeared; and the hermitage also disappeared at the same instant. And Musō Kokushi found himself kneeling alone in the high grass, beside an ancient and moss-grown tomb of the form called *go-rin-ishi,*[4] which seemed to be the tomb of a priest.

MUJINA

On the Akasaka Road, in Tōkyō, there is a slope called Kii-no-kuni-zaka—which means the Slope of the Province of Kii. I do not know why it is called the Slope of the Province of Kii. On one side of this slope you see an ancient moat, deep and very wide, with high green banks rising up to some place of gardens—and on the other side of the road extend the long and lofty walls of an imperial palace. Before the era of street-lamps and *jinrikishas*,[1] this neighborhood was very lonesome after dark; and belated pedestrians would go miles out of their way rather than mount the Kii-no-kuni-zaka, alone, after sunset.

All because of a Mujina that used to walk there.[2]

The last man who saw the Mujina was an old merchant of the Kyobashi quarter, who died about thirty years ago. This is the story, as he told it:

One night, at a late hour, he was hurrying up the Kii-no-kuni-zaka, when he perceived a woman crouching by the moat, all alone, and weeping bitterly.

Fearing that she intended to drown herself, he stopped to offer her any assistance or consolation in his power. She appeared to be a slight and graceful person, handsomely dressed; and her hair was arranged like that of a young girl of good family.

"O-jochū,"[3] he exclaimed, approaching her—"O-jochū, do not cry like that! ... Tell me what the trouble is; and if there be any way to help you, I shall be glad to help you." (He really meant what he said; for he was a very kind man.) But she continued to weep—hiding her face from him with one of her long sleeves.

"O-jochū," he said again, as gently as he could— "please, please listen to me! ... This is no place for a young lady at night! Do not cry, I implore you!—only tell me how I may be of some help to you!" Slowly she rose up, but turned her back to him, and continued to moan and sob behind her sleeve. He laid his hand lightly upon her shoulder, and pleaded: "O-jochū!—O-jochū!—O-jochū! ... Listen to me, just for one little moment! ... O-jochū!—O-jochū!" ... Then that O-jochū turned around, and dropped her sleeve, and stroked her face with her hand; and the man saw that she had no eyes or nose or mouth—and he screamed and ran away.[4]

Up Kii-no-kuni-zaka he ran and ran; and all was black and empty before him. On and on he ran, never daring to look back; and at last he saw a lantern, so far away that it looked like the gleam of a firefly; and he made for it. It proved to be only the lantern of an itinerant *soba*-seller,[5] who had set down his stand by the road-side; but any light and any human companionship was good after that experience; and he flung himself down at the feet of the soba-seller, crying out, "Ah!—aa!!—aa!!!"

"*Koré! koré!*"[6] roughly exclaimed the *soba*-man. "Here! What is the matter with you? Anybody hurt you?"

"No—nobody hurt me," panted the other—"only ... Ah!—aa!"

"—Only scared you?" queried the peddler, unsympathetically. "Robbers?"

"Not robbers—not robbers," gasped the terrified

man ... "I saw ... I saw a woman—by the moat; and she showed me ... Ah! I cannot tell you what she showed me!"

"He![7] Was it anything like THIS that she showed you?" cried the *soba*-man, stroking his own face—which therewith became like unto an Egg ... And, simultaneously, the light went out.

ROKURO-KUBI

Nearly five hundred years ago there was a samurai, named Isogai Héïdazaëmon Takétsura, in the service of the Lord Kikuji, of Kyūshū. This Isogai had inherited, from many warlike ancestors, a natural aptitude for military exercises, and extraordinary strength. While yet a boy he had surpassed his teachers in the art of swordsmanship, in archery, and in the use of the spear, and had displayed all the capacities of a daring and skillful soldier. Afterwards, in the time of the Eikyō [1] war, he so distinguished himself that high honors were bestowed upon him. But when the house of Kikuji came to ruin, Isogai found himself without a master. He might then easily have obtained service under another *daimyō*; but as he had never sought distinction for his own sake alone, and as his heart remained true to his former lord, he preferred to give up the world. So he cut off his hair, and became a traveling priest—taking the Buddhist name of Kwairyō.

But always, under the *koromo*[2] of the priest, Kwairyō kept warm within him the heart of the samurai. As in other years he had laughed at peril, so now also he scorned danger; and in all weathers and all seasons he journeyed to preach the good Law in places where no other priest would have dared to go. For that age was an age of violence and disorder; and upon the highways there was no security for the solitary traveler, even if he happened to be a priest.

In the course of his first long journey, Kwairyō had occasion to visit the province of Kai.[3] One evening, as he was traveling through the mountains of that province, darkness overcame him in a very lonesome district, leagues away from any village. So he resigned himself to pass the night under the stars; and having found a suitable grassy spot, by the roadside, he lay down there, and prepared to sleep. He had always welcomed discomfort; and even a bare rock was for him a good bed, when nothing better could be found, and the root of a pine-tree an excellent pillow. His body was iron; and he never troubled himself about dews or rain or frost or snow.

Scarcely had he lain down when a man came along the road, carrying an axe and a great bundle of chopped wood. This woodcutter halted on seeing Kwairyō lying down, and, after a moment of silent observation, said to him in a tone of great surprise:

"What kind of a man can you be, good Sir, that you dare to lie down alone in such a place as this? ... There are haunters about here—many of them. Are you not afraid of Hairy Things?"

"My friend," cheerfully answered Kwairyō, "I am only

a wandering priest—a 'Cloud-and-Water-Guest,' as folks call it: *Unsui-no-ryokaku*.[4] And I am not in the least afraid of Hairy Things—if you mean goblin-foxes, or goblin-badgers, or any creatures of that kind. As for lonesome places, I like them: they are suitable for meditation. I am accustomed to sleeping in the open air: and I have learned never to be anxious about my life."

"You must be indeed a brave man, Sir Priest," the peasant responded, "to lie down here! This place has a bad name—a very bad name. But, as the proverb has it, *Kunshi ayayuki ni chikayorazu* ['The superior man does not needlessly expose himself to peril']; and I must assure you, Sir, that it is very dangerous to sleep here. Therefore, although my house is only a wretched thatched hut, let me beg of you to come home with me at once. In the way of food, I have nothing to offer you; but there is a roof at least, and you can sleep under it without risk."

He spoke earnestly; and Kwairyō, liking the kindly tone of the man, accepted this modest offer. The wood-cutter guided him along a narrow path, leading up from the main road through mountain-forest. It was a rough and dangerous path—sometimes skirting precipices—sometimes offering nothing but a network of slippery roots for the foot to rest upon—sometimes winding over or between masses of jagged rock. But at last Kwairyō found himself upon a cleared space at the top of a hill, with a full moon shining overhead; and he saw before him a small thatched cottage, cheerfully lighted from within. The woodcutter led him to a shed at the back of the house, whither water had been conducted, through bamboo-pipes, from some neighboring stream; and the two men washed their feet. Beyond the shed was a vegetable garden, and a grove of cedars and bamboos; and beyond the trees appeared the glimmer of a cascade, pouring from some loftier height, and swaying in the moonshine like a long white robe.

As Kwairyō entered the cottage with his guide, he perceived four persons—men and women—warming their hands at a little fire kindled in the *ro*[5] of the principle apartment. They bowed low to the priest, and greeted him in the most respectful manner. Kwairyō wondered that persons so poor, and dwelling in such a solitude, should be aware of the polite forms of greeting.

"These are good people," he thought to himself; "and they must have been taught by someone well acquainted with the rules of propriety." Then turning to his host— the aruji, or house-master, as the others called him— Kwairyō said:

"From the kindness of your speech, and from the very polite welcome given me by your household, I imagine that you have not always been a woodcutter. Perhaps you formerly belonged to one of the upper classes?"

Smiling, the woodcutter answered:

"Sir, you are not mistaken. Though now living as you find me, I was once a person of some distinction. My story is the story of a ruined life—ruined by my own fault. I used to be in the service of a *daimyō*; and my rank in that service was not inconsiderable. But I loved women and wine too well; and under the influence of passion I acted wickedly. My selfishness brought about the ruin of our house, and caused the death of many persons. Retribution followed me; and I long remained a fugitive in the land.

Now I often pray that I may be able to make some atone-ment for the evil which I did, and to reestablish the ances-tral home. But I fear that I shall never find any way of so doing.

Nevertheless, I try to overcome the karma of my errors by sincere repentance, and by helping as far as I can, those who are unfortunate."

Kwairyō was pleased by this announcement of good resolve; and he said to the *aruji*:

"My friend, I have had occasion to observe that man, prone to folly in their youth, may in after years become very earnest in right living. In the holy sûtras it is written that those strongest in wrongdoing can become, by power of good resolve, the strongest in right-doing. I do not doubt that you have a good heart; and I hope that better fortune will come to you. To-night I shall recite the sûtras for your sake, and pray that you may obtain the force to overcome the karma of any past errors."

With these assurances, Kwairyō bade the *aruji* good-night; and his host showed him to a very small side-room, where a bed had been made ready. Then all went to sleep except the priest, who began to read the sutras by the light of a paper lantern. Until a late hour he continued to read and pray: then he opened a little window in his little sleeping-room, to take a last look at the landscape before lying down. The night was beautiful: there was no cloud in the sky: there was no wind; and the strong moonlight threw down sharp black shadows of foliage, and glittered on the dews of the garden. Shrillings of crickets and bell-insects[6] made a musical tumult; and the sound of the neighboring cascade deepened with the night. Kwairyō felt thirsty as he listened to the noise of the water; and, remembering the bamboo aqueduct at the rear of the house, he thought that he could go there and get a drink without disturbing the sleeping household. Very gently he pushed apart the sliding-screens that separated his room from the main apartment; and he saw, by the light of the lantern, five recumbent bodies—without heads!

For one instant he stood bewildered—imagining a crime. But in another moment he perceived that there was no blood, and that the headless necks did not look as if they had been cut. Then he thought to himself: "Either this is an illusion made by goblins, or I have been lured into the dwelling of a Rokuro-Kubi[7] ... In the book *Sōshinki* [8] it is written that if one find the body of a Rokuro-Kubi without its head, and remove the body to another place, the head will never be able to join itself again to the neck. And the book further says that when the head comes back and finds that its body has been moved, it will strike itself upon the floor three times—bounding like a ball—and will pant as in great fear, and presently die. Now, if these be Rokuro-Kubi, they mean me no good; so I shall be justified in following the instructions of the book."

He seized the body of the *aruji* by the feet, pulled it to the window, and pushed it out. Then he went to the back door, which he found barred; and he surmised that the heads had made their exit through the smoke-hole in the roof, which had been left open. Gently unbarring the door, he made his way to the garden, and proceeded with all possible caution to the grove beyond it. He heard voices talking in the grove; and he went in the direction of the voices—stealing from shadow to shadow, until he reached a good hiding-place. Then, from behind a trunk, he caught sight of the heads—all five of them—flitting about, and chatting as they flitted.

They were eating worms and insects which they found on the ground or among the trees. Presently the head of the *aruji* stopped eating and said:

"Ah, that traveling priest who came to-night!—how fat all his body is! When we shall have eaten him, our bellies will be well filled ... I was foolish to talk to him as I did; it only set him to reciting the sutras on behalf of my soul! To go near him while he is reciting would be difficult; and we cannot touch him so long as he is praying. But as it is now nearly morning, perhaps he has gone to sleep ... Some one of you go to the house and see what the fellow is doing."

Another head—the head of a young woman—immediately rose up and flitted to the house, lightly as a bat.

After a few minutes it came back, and cried out huskily, in a tone of great alarm:

"That traveling priest is not in the house; he is gone! But that is not the worst of the matter. He has taken the body of our *aruji*; and I do not know where he has put it."

At this announcement the head of the *aruji*—distinctly visible in the moonlight—assumed a frightful aspect: its eyes opened monstrously; its hair stood up bristling; and its teeth gnashed. Then a cry burst from its lips; and—weeping tears of rage—it exclaimed:

"Since my body has been moved, to rejoin it is not possible! Then I must die! ... And all through the work of that priest! Before I die I will get at that priest!—I will tear him!—I will devour him! ... AND THERE HE IS—behind that tree!—hiding behind that tree! See him!—the fat coward!"

In the same moment the head of the *aruji*, followed by the other four heads, sprang at Kwairyō. But the strong priest had already armed himself by plucking up a young tree; and with that tree he struck the heads as they came —knocking them from him with tremendous blows. Four of them fled away. But the head of the *aruji*, though battered again and again, desperately continued to bound at the priest, and at last caught him by the left sleeve of his robe. Kwairyō, however, as quickly gripped the head by its topknot, and repeatedly struck it. It did not release its hold; but it uttered a long moan, and thereafter ceased to struggle. It was dead. But its teeth still held the sleeve; and, for all his great strength, Kwairyō could not force open the jaws.

With the head still hanging to his sleeve he went back

to the house, and there caught sight of the other four
Rokuro-Kubi squatting together, with their bruised and
bleeding heads reunited to their bodies. But when they
perceived him at the back-door all screamed, "The priest!
the priest!"—and fled, through the other doorway, out
into the woods.

Eastward the sky was brightening; day was about to
dawn; and Kwairyō knew that the power of the goblins
was limited to the hours of darkness. He looked at the
head clinging to his sleeve—its face all fouled with blood
and foam and clay; and he laughed aloud as he thought to
himself: "What a *miyagé*![9]—the head of a goblin!" After
which he gathered together his few belongings, and
leisurely descended the mountain to continue his
journey.

Right on he journeyed, until he came to Suwa in
Shinano;[10] and into the main street of Suwa he solemnly
strode, with the head dangling at his elbow. Then woman
fainted, and children screamed and ran away; and there
was a great crowding and clamoring until the *torité* (as
the police in those days were called) seized the priest, and
took him to jail. For they supposed the head to be the
head of a murdered man who, in the moment of being
killed, had caught the murderer's sleeve in his teeth. As
the Kwairyō, he only smiled and said nothing when they
questioned him. So, after having passed a night in prison,
he was brought before the magistrates of the district.
Then he was ordered to explain how he, a priest, had been
found with the head of a man fastened to his sleeve, and
why he had dared thus shamelessly to parade his crime in
the sight of people.

Kwairyō laughed long and loudly at these questions; and then he said:

"Sirs, I did not fasten the head to my sleeve: it fastened itself there—much against my will. And I have not committed any crime. For this is not the head of a man; it is the head of a goblin; and, if I caused the death of the goblin, I did not do so by any shedding of blood, but simply by taking the precautions necessary to assure my own safety." And he proceeded to relate the whole of the adventure—bursting into another hearty laugh as he told of his encounter with the five heads.

But the magistrates did not laugh. They judged him to be a hardened criminal, and his story an insult to their intelligence. Therefore, without further questioning, they decided to order his immediate execution—all of them except one, a very old man. This aged officer had made no remark during the trial; but, after having heard the opinion of his colleagues, he rose up, and said:

"Let us first examine the head carefully; for this, I think, has not yet been done. If the priest has spoken truth, the head itself should bear witness for him ... Bring the head here!"

So the head, still holding in its teeth the *koromo* that had been stripped from Kwairyō's shoulders, was put before the judges. The old man turned it round and round, carefully examined it, and discovered, on the nape of its neck, several strange red characters. He called the attention of his colleagues to these, and also bade them observe that the edges of the neck nowhere presented the appearance of having been cut by any weapon. On the contrary, the line of leverance was smooth as the line at which a falling leaf detaches itself from the stem ... Then said the elder:

"I am quite sure that the priest told us nothing but the truth. This is the head of a Rokuro-Kubi. In the book Nan-ho-i-butsu-shi it is written that certain red characters can always be found upon the nape of the neck of a real Rokuro-Kubi. There are the characters: you can see for yourselves that they have not been painted. Moreover, it is well known that such goblins have been dwelling in the mountains of the province of Kai from very ancient time ... But you, Sir," he exclaimed, turning to Kwairyō—"what sort of sturdy priest may you be? Certainly you have given proof of a courage that few priests possess; and you have the air of a soldier rather than a priest. Perhaps you once belonged to the samurai-class?"

"You have guessed rightly, Sir," Kwairyō responded. "Before becoming a priest, I long followed the profession of arms; and in those days I never feared man or devil. My name then was Isogai Héïdazaëmon Takétsura of Kyūshū: there may be some among you who remember it."

At the mention of that name, a murmur of admiration filled the courtroom; for there were many present who remembered it. And Kwairyō immediately found himself among friends instead of judges—friends anxious to prove their admiration by fraternal kindness. With honor they escorted him to the residence of the *daimyō*, who welcomed him, and feasted him, and made him a handsome present before allowing him to depart. When Kwairyō left Suwa, he was as happy as any priest is permitted to be in this transitory world. As for the head, he took it with him—jocosely insisting that he intended it for a *miyagé*.

And now it only remains to tell what became of the head.

A day or two after leaving Suwa, Kwairyō met with a robber, who stopped him in a lonesome place, and bade him strip. Kwairyō at once removed his *koromo*, and offered it to the robber, who then first perceived what was hanging to the sleeve. Though brave, the highwayman was startled: he dropped the garment, and sprang back. Then he cried out:

"You!—what kind of a priest are you? Why, you are a worse man than I am! It is true that I have killed people; but I never walked about with anybody's head fastened to my sleeve ... Well, Sir priest, I suppose we are of the same calling; and I must say that I admire you! ... Now that head would be of use to me: I could frighten people with it. Will you sell it? You can have my robe in exchange for your *koromo*; and I will give you five *ryō* for the head."

Kwairyō answered:

"I shall let you have the head and the robe if you insist; but I must tell you that this is not the head of a man. It is a goblin's head. So, if you buy it, and have any trouble in consequence, please to remember that you were not deceived by me."

"What a nice priest you are!" exclaimed the robber. "You kill men, and jest about it! ... But I am really in earnest. Here is my robe; and here is the money; and let me have the head ... What is the use of joking?"

"Take the thing," said Kwairyō. "I was not joking. The only joke—if there be any joke at all—is that you are fool enough to pay good money for a goblin's head." And Kwairyō, loudly laughing, went upon his way.

Thus the robber got the head and the *koromo*; and for some time he played goblin-priest upon the highways. But, reaching the neighborhood of Suwa, he there leaned the true story of the head; and he then became afraid that the spirit of the Rokuro-Kubi might give him trouble. So he made up his mind to take back the head to the place from which it had come, and to bury it with its body. He found his way to the lonely cottage in the mountains of Kai; but nobody was there, and he could not discover the body. Therefore he buried the head by itself, in the grove behind the cottage; and he had a tombstone set up over the grave; and he caused a *Ségaki*-service to be performed on behalf of the spirit of the Rokuro-Kubi. And that tombstone—known as the Tombstone of the Rokuro-Kubi—may be seen (at least so the Japanese storyteller declares) even unto this day.

A DEAD SECRET

A long time ago, in the province of Tamba,[1] there lived a rich merchant named Inamuraya Gensuke. He had a daughter called O-Sono. As she was very clever and pretty, he thought it would be a pity to let her grow up with only such teaching as the country-teachers could give her: so he sent her, in care of some trusty attendants, to Kyoto, that she might be trained in the polite accomplishments taught to the ladies of the capital. After she had thus been educated, she was married to a friend of her father's family—a merchant named Nagaraya; and she lived happily with him for nearly four years. They had one child—a boy. But O-Sono fell ill and died, in the fourth year after her marriage.

On the night after the funeral of O-Sono, her little son said that his mamma had come back, and was in the room upstairs. She had smiled at him, but would not talk to him: so he became afraid, and ran away. Then some of the family went upstairs to the room which had been O-Sono's; and they were startled to see, by the light of a small lamp which had been kindled before a shrine in that room, the figure of the dead mother.

She appeared as if standing in front of a tansu, or chest of drawers, that still contained her ornaments and her wearing-apparel. Her head and shoulders could be very distinctly seen; but from the waist downwards the figure thinned into invisibility—it was like an imperfect reflection of her, and transparent as a shadow on water.

Then the folk were afraid, and left the room. Below they consulted together; and the mother of O-Sono's husband said:

"A woman is fond of her small things; and O-Sono was much attached to her belongings. Perhaps she has come back to look at them. Many dead persons will do that—unless the things be given to the parish-temple. If we present O-Sono's robes and girdles to the temple, her spirit will probably find rest."

It was agreed that this should be done as soon as possible. So on the following morning the drawers were emptied; and all of O-Sono's ornaments and dresses were taken to the temple. But she came back the next night, and looked at the tansu as before. And she came back also on the night following, and the night after that, and every night; and the house became a house of fear.

The mother of O-Sono's husband then went to the parish-temple, and told the chief priest all that had happened, and asked for ghostly counsel. The temple was a Zen temple; and the head-priest was a learned old man, known as Daigen Osho. He said:

"There must be something about which she is anxious, in or near that tansu."

"But we emptied all the drawers," replied the woman —"there is nothing in the tansu."

"Well," said Daigen Osho, "to-night I shall go to your house, and keep watch in that room, and see what can be done. You must give orders that no person shall enter the room while I am watching, unless I call."

After sundown, Daigen Osho went to the house, and found the room made ready for him. He remained there alone, reading the sûtras; and nothing appeared until after the Hour of the Rat.[2] Then the figure of O-Sono suddenly outlined itself in front of the tansu. Her face had a wistful look; and she kept her eyes fixed upon the tansu.

The priest uttered the holy formula prescribed in such

cases, and then, addressing the figure by the kaimyo[3] of O-Sono, said:

"I have come here in order to help you. Perhaps in that tansu there is something about which you have reason to feel anxious. Shall I try to find it for you?" The shadow appeared to give assent by a slight motion of the head; and the priest, rising, opened the top drawer. It was empty. Successively he opened the second, the third, and the fourth drawer—he searched carefully behind them and beneath them—he carefully examined the interior of the chest. He found nothing. But the figure remained gazing as wistfully as before. "What can she want?" thought the priest.

Suddenly it occurred to him that there might be something hidden under the paper with which the drawers were lined. He removed the lining of the first drawer—nothing! He removed the lining of the second and third drawers—still nothing. But under the lining of the lowermost drawer he found—a letter.

"Is this the thing about which you have been troubled?" he asked. The shadow of the woman turned toward him—her faint gaze fixed upon the letter. "Shall I burn it for you?" he asked. She bowed before him. "It shall be burned in the temple this very morning," he promised —"and no one shall read it, except myself." The figure smiled and vanished.

Dawn was breaking as the priest descended the stairs, to find the family waiting anxiously below. "Do not be anxious," he said to them: "She will not appear again." And she never did.

The letter was burned. It was a love-letter written to O-Sono in the time of her studies at Kyoto. But the priest alone knew what was in it; and the secret died with him.

YUKI-ONNA

In a village of Musashi Province,[1] there lived two woodcutters: Mosaku and Minokichi. At the time of which I am speaking, Mosaku was an old man; and Minokichi, his apprentice, was a lad of eighteen years. Every day they went together to a forest situated about five miles from their village. On the way to that forest there is a wide river to cross; and there is a ferryboat. Several times a bridge was built where the ferry is; but the bridge was each time carried away by a flood. No common bridge can resist the current there when the river rises.

Mosaku and Minokichi were on their way home, one very cold evening, when a great snowstorm overtook them. They reached the ferry; and they found that the boatman had gone away, leaving his boat on the other side of the river. It was no day for swimming; and the woodcutters took shelter in the ferryman's hut—thinking

73

themselves lucky to find any shelter at all. There was no brazier in the hut, nor any place in which to make a fire: it was only a two-mat hut,[2] with a single door, but no window. Mosaku and Minokichi fastened the door, and lay down to rest, with their straw raincoats over them. At first they did not feel very cold; and they thought that the storm would soon be over.

The old man almost immediately fell asleep; but the boy, Minokichi, lay awake a long time, listening to the awful wind, and the continual slashing of the snow against the door. The river was roaring; and the hut swayed and creaked like a junk at sea. It was a terrible storm; and the air was every moment becoming colder; and Minokichi shivered under his raincoat. But at last, in spite of the cold, he too fell asleep.

He was awakened by a showering of snow in his face. The door of the hut had been forced open; and, by the snow-light (*yuki-akari*), he saw a woman in the room—a woman all in white. She was bending above Mosaku, and blowing her breath upon him; and her breath was like a bright white smoke. Almost in the same moment she turned to Minokichi, and stooped over him. He tried to cry out, but found that he could not utter any sound. The white woman bent down over him, lower and lower, until her face almost touched him; and he saw that she was very beautiful—though her eyes made him afraid. For a little time she continued to look at him; then she smiled, and she whispered:

"I intended to treat you like the other man. But I cannot help feeling some pity for you—because you are so young ... You are a pretty boy, Minokichi; and I will not hurt you now. But, if you ever tell anybody—even your own mother—about what you have seen this night, I shall know it; and then I will kill you ... Remember what I say!"

With these words, she turned from him, and passed through the doorway. Then he found himself able to move; and he sprang up, and looked out. But the woman was nowhere to be seen; and the snow was driving furiously into the hut. Minokichi closed the door, and secured it by fixing several billets of wood against it.

He wondered if the wind had blown it open; he

thought that he might have been only dreaming, and might have mistaken the gleam of the snow-light in the doorway for the figure of a white woman: but he could not be sure. He called to Mosaku, and was frightened because the old man did not answer. He put out his hand in the dark, and touched Mosaku's face, and found that it was ice! Mosaku was stark and dead.

By dawn the storm was over; and when the ferryman returned to his station, a little after sunrise, he found Minokichi lying senseless beside the frozen body of Mosaku. Minokichi was promptly cared for, and soon came to himself; but he remained a long time ill from the effects of the cold of that terrible night.

He had been greatly frightened also by the old man's death; but he said nothing about the vision of the woman in white. As soon as he got well again, he returned to his calling—going alone every morning to the forest, and coming back at nightfall with his bundles of wood, which his mother helped him to sell.

One evening, in the winter of the following year, as he was on his way home, he overtook a girl who happened to be traveling by the same road. She was a tall, slim girl, very good-looking; and she answered Minokichi's greeting in a voice as pleasant to the ear as the voice of a songbird. Then he walked beside her; and they began to talk. The girl said that her name was O-Yuki;[3] that she had lately lost both of her parents; and that she was going to Yedo,[4] were she happened to have some poor relations, who might help her to find a situation as a servant.

Minokichi soon felt charmed by this strange girl; and

the more that he looked at her, the handsomer she appeared to be. He asked her whether she was yet betrothed; and she answered, laughingly, that she was free. Then, in her turn, she asked Minokichi whether he was married, or pledged to marry; and he told her that, although he had only a widowed mother to support, the question of an "honorable daughter-in-law" had not yet been considered, as he was very young ... After these confidences, they walked on for a long while without speaking; but, as the proverb declares, *Ki ga aréba, mé mo kuchi hodo ni mono wo iu*: "When the wish is there, the eyes can say as much as the mouth."

By the time they reached the village, they had become very much pleased with each other; and then Minokichi asked O-Yuki to rest awhile at his house.

After some shy hesitation, she went there with him; and his mother made her welcome, and prepared a warm meal for her. O-Yuki behaved so nicely that Minokichi's mother took a sudden fancy to her, and persuaded her to delay her journey to Yedo. And the natural end of the matter was that Yuki never went to Yedo at all. She remained in the house, as an "honorable daughter-in-law."

O-Yuki proved a very good daughter-in-law. When Minokichi's mother came to die—some five years later— her last words were words of affection and praise for the wife of her son. And O-Yuki bore Minokichi ten children, boys and girls—handsome children all of them, and very fair of skin.

The country-folk thought O-Yuki a wonderful person,

by nature different from themselves. Most of the peasant-women age early; but O-Yuki, even after having become the mother of ten children, looked as young and fresh as on the day when she had first come to the village.

One night, after the children had gone to sleep, O-Yuki was sewing by the light of a paper lamp; and Mino-kichi, watching her, said:

"To see you sewing there, with the light on your face, makes me think of a strange thing that happened when I was a lad of eighteen. I then saw somebody as beautiful and white as you are now—indeed, she was very like you."

Without lifting her eyes from her work, O-Yuki responded:

"Tell me about her ... Where did you see her?"

Then Minokichi told her about the terrible night in the ferryman's hut—and about the White Woman that had stooped above him, smiling and whispering—and about the silent death of old Mosaku. And he said:

"Asleep or awake, that was the only time that I saw a being as beautiful as you. Of course, she was not a human being; and I was afraid of her—very much afraid—but she was so white! ... Indeed, I have never been sure whether it was a dream that I saw, or the Woman of the Snow."

O-Yuki flung down her sewing, and arose, and bowed above Minokichi where he sat, and shrieked into his face:

"It was I—I—I! Yuki it was! And I told you then that I would kill you if you ever said one word about it! ... But for those children asleep there, I would kill you this moment! And now you had better take very, very good care of them;

for if ever they have reason to complain of you, I will treat you as you deserve!"

Even as she screamed, her voice became thin, like a crying of wind; then she melted into a bright white mist that spired to the roof-beams, and shuddered away through the smoke-hold ... Never again was she seen.

THE STORY OF AOYAGI

I n the era of Bummei [1469–1486] there was a young samurai called Tomotada in the service of Hatakéyama Yoshimuné, the Lord of Noto.[1] Tomo-tada was a native of Echizen,[2] but at an early age he had been taken, as page, into the palace of the *daimyō* of Noto, and had been educated, under the supervision of that prince, for the profession of arms. As he grew up, he proved himself both a good scholar and a good soldier, and continued to enjoy the favor of his prince. Being gifted with an amiable character, a winning address, and a very handsome person, he was admired and much liked by his samurai-comrades.

When Tomotada was about twenty years old, he was sent upon a private mission to Hosokawa Masamoto, the great *daimyō* of Kyōto, a kinsman of Hatakéyama Yoshimuné. Having been ordered to journey through Echizen, the youth requested and obtained permission to pay a visit, on the way, to his widowed mother.

It was the coldest period of the year when he started; and, though mounted upon a powerful horse, he found himself obliged to proceed slowly. The road which he followed passed through a mountain-district where the settlements were few and far between; and on the second day of his journey, after a weary ride of hours, he was dismayed to find that he could not reach his intended halting-place until late in the night. He had reason to be anxious; for a heavy snowstorm came on, with an intensely cold wind; and the horse showed signs of exhaustion. But in that trying moment, Tomotada unexpectedly perceived the thatched room of a cottage on the summit of a near hill, where willow-trees were growing. With difficulty he urged his tired animal to the dwelling; and he loudly knocked upon the storm-doors, which had been closed against the wind. An old woman opened them, and cried out compassionately at the sight of the handsome stranger: "Ah, how pitiful!—a young gentleman traveling alone in such weather! ... Deign, young master, to enter."

Tomotada dismounted, and after leading his horse to a shed in the rear, entered the cottage, where he saw an old man and a girl warming themselves by a fire of bamboo splints. They respectfully invited him to approach the fire; and the old folks then proceeded to warm some rice-wine, and to prepare food for the traveler, whom they ventured to question in regard to his journey. Meanwhile the young girl disappeared behind a screen. Tomotada had observed, with astonishment, that she was extremely beautiful—though her attire was of the most wretched kind, and her long, loose hair in disorder. He wondered that so handsome a girl should be living in such a miserable and lonesome place.

The old man said to him:

"Honored Sir, the next village is far; and the snow is falling thickly. The wind is piercing; and the road is very bad. Therefore, to proceed further this night would probably be dangerous. Although this hovel is unworthy of your presence, and although we have not any comfort to offer, perhaps it were safer to remain to-night under this miserable roof ... We would take good care of your horse."

Tomotada accepted this humble proposal—secretly glad of the chance thus afforded him to see more of the young girl. Presently a coarse but ample meal was set before him; and the girl came from behind the screen, to serve the wine. She was now reclad, in a rough but cleanly robe of homespun; and her long, loose hair had been neatly combed and smoothed. As she bent forward to fill his cup, Tomotada was amazed to perceive that she was incomparably more beautiful than any woman whom he had ever before seen; and there was a grace about her every motion that astonished him. But the elders began to apologize for her, saying:

"Sir, our daughter, Aoyagi,[3] has been brought up here in the mountains, almost alone; and she knows nothing of gentle service. We pray that you will pardon her stupidity and her ignorance." Tomotada protested that he deemed himself lucky to be waited upon by so comely a maiden. He could not turn his eyes away from her— though he saw that his admiring gaze made her blush; and he left the wine and food untasted before him. The mother said: "Kind Sir, we very much hope that you will try to eat and to drink a little—though our peasant-fare is of the worst—as you must have been chilled by that piercing wind." Then, to please the old folks, Tomotada ate and drank as he could; but the charm of the blushing girl still grew upon him. He talked with her, and found that her speech was sweet as her face. Brought up in the mountains as she might have been; but, in that case, her parents must at some time been persons of high degree; for she spoke and moved like a damsel of rank. Suddenly he addressed her with a poem—which was also a question—inspired by the delight in his heart:

> *"Tadzunetsuru,*
> *Hana ka tote koso,*
> *Hi wo kurase,*
> *Akenu ni otoru*
> *Akane sasuran?"*

["Being on my way to pay a visit, I found that which I took to be a flower: therefore here I spend the day ... Why, in the time before dawn, the dawn-blush tint should glow —that, indeed, I know not."][4]

Without a moment's hesitation, she answered him in these verses:

> *"Izuru hi no*
> *Honomeku iro wo*
> *Waga sode ni*
> *Tsutsumaba asu mo*
> *Kimiya tomaran."*

84

["If with my sleeve I hid the faint fair color of the dawning sun—then, perhaps, in the morning my lord will remain."][5]

Then Tomotada knew that she accepted his admiration; and he was scarcely less surprised by the art with which she had uttered her feelings in verse, than delighted by the assurance which the verses conveyed. He was now certain that in all this world he could not hope to meet, much less to win, a girl more beautiful and witty than this rustic maid before him; and a voice in his heart seemed to cry out urgently, "Take the luck that the gods have put in your way!" In short he was bewitched—bewitched to such a degree that, without further preliminary, he asked the old people to give him their daughter in marriage—telling them, at the same time, his name and lineage, and his rank in the train of the Lord of Noto.

They bowed down before him, with many exclamations of grateful astonishment. But, after some moments of apparent hesitation, the father replied:

"Honored master, you are a person of high position, and likely to rise to still higher things. Too great is the favor that you deign to offer us; indeed, the depth of our gratitude therefore is not to be spoken or measured. But this girl of ours, being a stupid country-girl of vulgar birth, with no training or teaching of any sort, it would be improper to let her become the wife of a noble samurai. Even to speak of such a matter is not right ... But, since you find the girl to your liking, and have condescended to pardon her peasant-manners and to overlook her great rudeness, we do gladly present her to you, for an humble handmaid. Deign, therefore, to act hereafter in her regard according to your august pleasure."

Ere morning the storm had passed; and day broke through a cloudless east. Even if the sleeve of Aoyagi hid from her lover's eyes the rose-blush of that dawn, he could no longer tarry. But neither could he resign himself to part with the girl; and, when everything had been prepared for his journey, he thus addressed her parents:

"Though it may seem thankless to ask for more than I have already received, I must again beg you to give me your daughter for wife. It would be difficult for me to separate from her now; and as she is willing to accompany me, if you permit, I can take her with me as she is. If you will give her to me, I shall ever cherish you as parents ... And, in the meantime, please to accept this poor acknowledgment of your kindest hospitality."

So saying, he placed before his humble host a purse of gold *ryō*. But the old man, after many prostrations, gently pushed back the gift, and said:

"Kind master, the gold would be of no use to us; and you will probably have need of it during your long, cold journey. Here we buy nothing; and we could not spend so much money upon ourselves, even if we wished ... As for the girl, we have already bestowed her as a free gift; she belongs to you: therefore it is not necessary to ask our leave to take her away. Already she has told us that she hopes to accompany you, and to remain your servant for as long as you may be willing to endure her presence. We are only too happy to know that you deign to accept her; and we pray that you will not trouble yourself on our account. In this place we could not provide her with proper clothing—much less with a dowry. Moreover, being old, we should in any event have to separate from her before long. Therefore it is very fortunate that you should be willing to take her with you now."

It was in vain that Tomotada tried to persuade the old people to accept a present: he found that they cared nothing for money. But he saw that they were really anxious to trust their daughter's fate to his hands; and he therefore decided to take her with him. So he placed her upon his horse, and bade the old folks farewell for the time being, with many sincere expressions of gratitude.

"Honored Sir," the father made answer, "it is we, and not you, who have reason for gratitude. We are sure that you will be kind to our girl; and we have no fears for her sake."

[Here, in the Japanese original, there is a queer break in the natural course of the narration, which therefrom remains curiously inconsistent. Nothing further is said about the mother of Tomotada, or about the parents of Aoyagi, or about the daimyō of Noto. Evidently the writer wearied of his work at this point, and hurried the story, very carelessly, to its startling end. I am not able to supply his omissions, or to repair his faults of construction; but I must venture to put in a few explanatory details, without which the rest of the tale would not hold together ... It appears that Tomotada rashly took Aoyagi with him to Kyōto, and so got into trouble; but we are not informed as to where the couple lived afterwards.]

Now a samurai was not allowed to marry without the consent of his lord; and Tomotada could not expect to obtain this sanction before his mission had been accomplished. He had reason, under such circumstances, to fear that the beauty of Aoyagi might attract dangerous attention, and that means might be devised of taking her away from him. In Kyōto he therefore tried to keep her hidden from curious eyes. But a retainer of Lord Hosokawa one day caught sight of Aoyagi, discovered her relation to Tomotada, and reported the matter to the *daimyō*. Thereupon the *daimyō*—a young prince, and fond of pretty faces—gave orders that the girl should be brought to the place; and she was taken thither at once, without ceremony.

Tomotada sorrowed unspeakably; but he knew himself powerless. He was only an humble messenger in the service of a far-off *daimyō*; and for the time being he was at the mercy of a much more powerful *daimyō*, whose wishes were not to be questioned. Moreover Tomotada knew that he had acted foolishly—that he had brought about his own misfortune, by entering into a clandestine relation which the code of the military class condemned. There was now but one hope for him—a desperate hope: that Aoyagi might be able and willing to escape and to flee with him. After long reflection, he resolved to try to send her a letter. The attempt would be dangerous, of course: any writing sent to her might find its way to the hands of the *daimyō*; and to send a love-letter to any inmate of the place was an unpardonable offense. But he resolved to dare the risk; and, in the form of a Chinese poem, he composed a letter which he endeavored to have conveyed to her. The poem was written with only twenty-eight characters. But with those twenty-eight characters he was about to express all the depth of his passion, and to suggest all the pain of his loss:[6]

Kōshi ō-son gojin wo ou;
Ryokuju namida wo tarété rakin wo hitataru;
Komon hitotabi irité fukaki koto umi no gotoshi;
Koré yori shorō koré rojin

[*Closely, closely the youthful prince now follows after the gem-bright maid; The tears of the fair one, falling, have moistened all her robes. But the august lord, having once become enamored of her—the depth of his longing is like the depth of the sea.*

Therefore it is only I that am left forlorn—only I that am left to wander along.]

On the evening of the day after this poem had been sent, Tomotada was summoned to appear before the Lord Hosokawa. The youth at once suspected that his confidence had been betrayed; and he could not hope, if his letter had been seen by the *daimyō*, to escape the severest penalty. "Now he will order my death," thought Tomotada; "but I do not care to live unless Aoyagi be restored to me. Besides, if the death-sentence be passed, I can at least try to kill Hosokawa." He slipped his swords into his girdle, and hastened to the palace.

On entering the presence-room he saw the Lord Hosokawa seated upon the dais, surrounded by samurai of high rank, in caps and robes of ceremony. All were silent as statues; and while Tomotada advanced to make obeisance, the hush seemed to his sinister and heavy, like the stillness before a storm. But Hosokawa suddenly descended from the dais, and, while taking the youth by the arm, began to repeat the words of the poem: *"Kōshi ō-*

son gojin wo ou." ... And Tomotada, looking up, saw kindly
tears in the prince's eyes.

Then said Hosokawa:

"Because you love each other so much, I have taken it
upon myself to authorize your marriage, in lieu of my
kinsman, the Lord of Noto; and your wedding shall now
be celebrated before me. The guests are assembled; the
gifts are ready."

At a signal from the lord, the sliding-screens

concealing a further apartment were pushed open; and Tomotada saw there many dignitaries of the court, assembled for the ceremony, and Aoyagi awaiting him in brides' apparel ... Thus was she given back to him; and the wedding was joyous and splendid; and precious gifts were made to the young couple by the prince, and by the members of his household.

For five happy years, after that wedding, Tomotada and Aoyagi dwelt together. But one morning Aoyagi, while talking with her husband about some household matter, suddenly uttered a great cry of pain, and then became very white and still. After a few moments she said, in a feeble voice: "Pardon me for thus rudely crying out—but the pain was so sudden! ... My dear husband, our union must have been brought about through some Karma-relation in a former state of existence; and that happy relation, I think, will bring us again together in more than one life to come. But for this present existence of ours, the relation is now ended;—we are about to be separated. Repeat for me, I beseech you, the *Nembutsu*-prayer—because I am dying."

"Oh! What strange wild fancies!" cried the startled husband—"you are only a little unwell, my dear one! ... lie down for a while, and rest; and the sickness will pass."

"No, no!" she responded—"I am dying!—I do not imagine it; I know! ... And it were needless now, my dear husband, to hide the truth from you any longer: I am not a human being. The soul of a tree is my soul; the heart of a tree is my heart; the sap of the willow is my life. And some one, at this cruel moment, is cutting down my tree; that is why I must die! ... Even to weep were now beyond my strength!—quickly, quickly repeat the *Nembutsu* for me ... quickly! ... Ah...!"

With another cry of pain she turned aside her beautiful head, and tried to hide her face behind her sleeve. But almost in the same moment her whole form appeared to collapse in the strangest way, and to sink down, down, down—level with the floor. Tomotada had sprung to support her; but there was nothing to support! There lay on the matting only the empty robes of the fair creature and the ornaments that she had worn in her hair: the body had ceased to exist.

Tomotada shaved his head, took the Buddhist vows, and became an itinerant priest. He traveled through all the provinces of the empire; and, at holy places which he visited, he offered up prayers for the soul of Aoyagi. Reaching Echizen, in the course of his pilgrimage, he sought the home of the parents of his beloved. But when he arrived at the lonely place among the hills, where their dwelling had been, he found that the cottage had disappeared. There was nothing to mark even the spot where it had stood, except the stumps of three willows—two old trees and one young tree—that had been cut down long before his arrival.

Beside the stumps of those willow-trees he erected a memorial tomb, inscribed with divers holy texts; and he there performed many Buddhist services on behalf of the spirits of Aoyagi and of her parents.

JIU-ROKU-ZAKURA

In Wakegori, a district of the province of Iyo,[1] there
is a very ancient and famous cherry-tree, called Jiu-
roku-zakura, or "the Cherry-tree of the Sixteenth
Day," because it blooms every year upon the sixteenth day
of the first month (by the old lunar calendar)—and only
upon that day. Thus the time of its flowering is the Period
of Great Cold—though the natural habit of a cherry-tree
is to wait for the spring season before venturing to blossom. But the Jiu-roku-zakura blossoms with a life that is
not—or, at least, that was not originally—its own. There
is the ghost of a man in that tree.

He was a samurai of Iyo; and the tree grew in his
garden; and it used to flower at the usual time—that is to
say, about the end of March or the beginning of April. He
had played under that tree when he was a child; and his
parents and grandparents and ancestors had hung to its
blossoming branches, season after season for more than a

95

hundred years, bright strips of colored paper inscribed with poems of praise.

He himself became very old—outliving all his children; and there was nothing in the world left for him to live except that tree. And lo! In the summer of a certain year, the tree withered and died!

Exceedingly the old man sorrowed for his tree. Then kind neighbors found for him a young and beautiful cherry-tree, and planted it in his garden—hoping thus to comfort him. And he thanked them, and pretended to be glad. But really his heart was full of pain; for he had loved the old tree so well that nothing could have consoled him for the loss of it.

At last there came to him a happy thought: he remembered a way by which the perishing tree might be saved. (It was the sixteenth day of the first month.) Along he went into his garden, and bowed down before the withered tree, and spoke to it, saying: "Now deign, I beseech you, once more to bloom—because I am going to die in your stead." (For it is believed that one can really give away one's life to another person, or to a creature or even to a tree, by the favor of the gods; and thus to transfer one's life is expressed by the term *migawari ni tatsu*, "to act as a substitute.") Then under that tree he spread a white cloth, and divers coverings, and sat down upon the coverings, and performed *hara-kiri* after the fashion of a samurai. And the ghost of him went into the tree, and made it blossom in that same hour.

And every year it still blooms on the sixteenth day of the first month, in the season of snow.

THE DREAM
OF AKINOSUKÉ

I n the district called Toïchi of Yamato Province,[1]
there used to live a *gōshi* named Miyata
Akinosuké ... [Here I must tell you that in Japanese
feudal times there was a privileged class of soldier-
farmers—free-holders—corresponding to the class of
yeomen in England; and these were called *gōshi*.]

In Akinosuké's garden there was a great and ancient
cedar-tree, under which he was wont to rest on sultry
days. One very warm afternoon he was sitting under this
tree with two of his friends, fellow- *gōshi*, chatting and
drinking wine, when he felt all of a sudden very drowsy—
so drowsy that he begged his friends to excuse him for
taking a nap in their presence. Then he lay down at the
foot of the tree, and dreamed this dream:

He thought that as he was lying there in his garden,
he saw a procession, like the train of some great *daimyō*
descending a hill nearby, and that he got up to look at it. A
very grand procession it proved to be—more imposing

than anything of the kind which he had ever seen before; and it was advancing toward his dwelling. He observed in the van of it a number of young men richly appareled, who were drawing a great lacquered palace-carriage, or *gosho-guruma*, hung with bright blue silk. When the procession arrived within a short distance of the house it halted; and a richly dressed man—evidently a person of rank—advanced from it, approached Akinosuké, bowed to him profoundly, and then said:

"Honored Sir, you see before you a *kérai* [vassal] of the Kokuō of Tokoy.[2] [My master, the King, commands me to greet you in his august name, and to place myself wholly at your disposal. He also bids me inform you that he augustly desires your presence at the palace. Be therefore pleased immediately to enter this honorable carriage, which he has sent for your conveyance."

Upon hearing these words Akinosuké wanted to make some fitting reply; but he was too much astonished and embarrassed for speech; and in the same moment his will seemed to melt away from him, so that he could only do as the *kérai* bade him. He entered the carriage; the *kérai* took a place beside him, and made a signal; the drawers, seizing the silken ropes, turned the great vehicle southward; and the journey began.

In a very short time, to Akinosuké's amazement, the carriage stopped in front of a huge two-storied gateway (*romōn*), of a Chinese style, which he had never before seen. Here the *kérai* dismounted, saying, "I go to announce the honorable arrival,"—and he disappeared. After some little waiting, Akinosuké saw two noble-looking men, wearing robes of purple silk and high caps of the form indicating lofty rank, come from the gate-way. These, after having respectfully saluted him, helped him to descend from the carriage, and led him through the great gate and across a vast garden, to the entrance of a palace whose front appeared to extend, west and east, to a distance of miles. Akinosuké was then shown into a reception-room of wonderful size and splendor. His guides conducted him to the place of honor, and respectfully seated themselves apart; while serving-maids, in costume of ceremony, brought refreshments. When Akinosuké had partaken of the refreshments, the two purple-robed attendants bowed low before him, and addressed him in the following words—each speaking alternately, according to the etiquette of courts:

"It is now our honorable duty to inform you ... as to the reason of your having been summoned hither ... Our master, the King, augustly desires that you become his son-in-law; ... and it is his wish and command that you shall wed this very day ... the August Princess, his maiden-daughter ... We shall soon conduct you to the presence-chamber ... where His Augustness even now is waiting to receive you ... But it will be necessary that we first invest you ... with the appropriate garments of ceremony."[3]

Having thus spoken, the attendants rose together, and proceeded to an alcove containing a great chest of gold lacquer. They opened the chest, and took from it various robes and girdles of rich material, and a *kamuri*, or regal headdress. With these they attired Akinosuké as befitted a princely bridegroom; and he was then conducted to the presence-room, where he saw the Kokuō of Tokoyo seated upon the daiza,[4] wearing a high black cap of state, and robed in robes of yellow silk.

Before the daiza, to left and right, a multitude of dignitaries sat in rank, motionless and splendid as images in a temple; and Akinosuké, advancing into their midst, saluted the king with the triple prostration of usage. The king greeted him with gracious words, and then said:

"You have already been informed as to the reason of your having been summoned to Our presence. We have decided that you shall become the adopted husband of Our only daughter; and the wedding ceremony shall now be performed."

As the king finished speaking, a sound of joyful music was heard; and a long train of beautiful court ladies advanced from behind a curtain to conduct Akinosuké to the room in which his bride awaited him.

The room was immense; but it could scarcely contain

the multitude of guests assembled to witness the wedding ceremony. All bowed down before Akinosuké as he took his place, facing the King's daughter, on the kneeling-cushion prepared for him. As a maiden of heaven the bride appeared to be; and her robes were beautiful as a summer sky. And the marriage was performed amid great rejoicing.

Afterwards the pair were conducted to a suite of apartments that had been prepared for them in another portion of the palace; and there they received the congratulations of many noble persons, and wedding gifts beyond counting.

Some days later Akinosuké was again summoned to the throne-room. On this occasion he was received even more graciously than before; and the King said to him:

"In the southwestern part of Our dominion there is an island called Raishū. We have now appointed you Governor of that island. You will find the people loyal and docile; but their laws have not yet been brought into proper accord with the laws of Tokoyo; and their customs have not been properly regulated. We entrust you with the duty of improving their social condition as far as may be possible; and We desire that you shall rule them with kindness and wisdom. All preparations necessary for your journey to Raishū have already been made."

So Akinosuké and his bride departed from the palace of Tokoyo, accompanied to the shore by a great escort of nobles and officials; and they embarked upon a ship of state provided by the king. And with favoring winds they safety sailed to Raishū, and found the good people of that island assembled upon the beach to welcome them.

Akinosuké entered at once upon his new duties; and they did not prove to be hard. During the first three years of his governorship he was occupied chiefly with the framing and the enactment of laws; but he had wise counselors to help him, and he never found the work unpleasant. When it was all finished, he had no active duties to perform, beyond attending the rites and ceremonies ordained by ancient custom. The country was so healthy and so fertile that sickness and want were unknown; and the people were so good that no laws were ever broken. And Akinosuké dwelt and ruled in Raishū for twenty years more—making in all twenty-three years of sojourn, during which no shadow of sorrow traversed his life.

But in the twenty-fourth year of his governorship, a great misfortune came upon him; for his wife, who had borne him seven children—five boys and two girls—fell sick and died. She was buried, with high pomp, on the summit of a beautiful hill in the district of Hanryoko; and a monument, exceedingly splendid, was placed upon her grave. But Akinosuké felt such grief at her death that he no longer cared to live.

Now when the legal period of mourning was over, there came to Raishū, from the Tokoyo palace, a *shisha*, or royal messenger. The *shisha* delivered to Akinosuké a message of condolence, and then said to him:

"These are the words which our august master, the King of Tokoyo, commands that I repeat to you: 'We will now send you back to your own people and country. As for the seven children, they are the grandsons and granddaughters of the King, and shall be fitly cared for. Do not, therefore, allow your mind to be troubled concerning them.'"

On receiving this mandate, Akinosuké submissively prepared for his departure. When all his affairs had been settled, and the ceremony of bidding farewell to his counselors and trusted officials had been concluded, he was escorted with much honor to the port.

There he embarked upon the ship sent for him; and the ship sailed out into the blue sea, under the blue sky; and the shape of the island of Raishū itself turned blue, and then turned grey, and then vanished forever ... And Akinosuké suddenly awoke—under the cedar-tree in his own garden!

For a moment he was stupefied and dazed. But he perceived his two friends still seated near him—drinking and chatting merrily. He stared at them in a bewildered way, and cried aloud, "How strange!"

"Akinosuké must have been dreaming," one of them exclaimed, with a laugh. "What did you see, Akinosuké, that was strange?"

Then Akinosuké told his dream—that dream of three-and-twenty years' sojourn in the realm of Tokoyo, in the island of Raishū; and they were astonished, because he had really slept for no more than a few minutes.

One gōshi said:

"Indeed, you saw strange things. We also saw something strange while you were napping. A little yellow butterfly was fluttering over your face for a moment or two; and we watched it. Then it alighted on the ground beside you, close to the tree; and almost as soon as it alighted there, a big, big ant came out of a hole and seized it and pulled it down into the hole. Just before you woke up, we saw that very butterfly come out of the hole again, and flutter over your face as before. And then it suddenly disappeared: we do not know where it went."

"Perhaps it was Akinosuké's soul," the other gōshi said; "certainly I thought I saw it fly into his mouth ... But, even if that butterfly was Akinosuké's soul, the fact would not explain his dream."

"The ants might explain it," returned the first speaker. "Ants are queer beings—possibly goblins ... Anyhow, there is a big ant's nest under that cedar-tree."

"Let us look!" cried Akinosuké, greatly moved by this suggestion. And he went for a spade.

The ground about and beneath the cedar-tree proved to have been excavated, in a most surprising way, by a prodigious colony of ants. The ants had furthermore built inside their excavations; and their tiny constructions of straw, clay, and stems bore an odd resemblance to miniature towns. In the middle of a structure considerably larger than the rest there was a marvelous swarming of small ants around the body of one very big ant, which had yellowish wings and a long black head.

"Why, there is the King of my dream!" cried Akinosuké; "and there is the palace of Tokoyo! ... How extraordinary! ... Raishū ought to lie somewhere southwest of it—to the left of that big root ... Yes!—here it is! ... How very strange! Now I am sure that I can find the mountain of Hanryoko, and the grave of the princess."

In the wreck of the nest he searched and searched, and at last discovered a tiny mound, on the top of which was fixed a water-worn pebble, in shape resembling a Buddhist monument. Underneath it he found— embedded in clay—the dead body of a female ant.

RIKI-BAKA

His name was Riki, signifying Strength; but the people called him Riki-the-Simple, or Riki-the-Fool,—"Riki-Baka,"—because he had been born into perpetual childhood. For the same reason they were kind to him—even when he set a house on fire by putting a lighted match to a mosquito-curtain, and clapped his hands for joy to see the blaze. At sixteen years he was a tall, strong lad; but in mind he remained always at the happy age of two, and therefore continued to play with very small children.

The bigger children of the neighborhood, from four to seven years old, did not care to play with him, because he could not learn their songs and games. His favorite toy was a broomstick, which he used as a hobbyhorse; and for hours at a time he would ride on that broomstick, up and down the slope in front of my house, with amazing peals of laughter. But at last he became troublesome by reason of his noise; and I had to tell him that he must find another playground.

He bowed submissively, and then went off,—sorrowfully trailing his broomstick behind him. Gentle at all times, and perfectly harmless if allowed no chance to play with fire, he seldom gave anybody cause for complaint. His relation to the life of our street was scarcely more than that of a dog or a chicken; and when he finally disappeared, I did not miss him. Months and months passed by before anything happened to remind me of Riki.

"What has become of Riki?" I then asked the old woodcutter who supplies our neighborhood with fuel. I remembered that Riki had often helped him to carry his bundles.

"Riki-Baka?" answered the old man. "Ah, Riki is dead —poor fellow! ... Yes, he died nearly a year ago, very suddenly; the doctors said that he had some disease of the brain. And there is a strange story now about that poor Riki.

"When Riki died, his mother wrote his name, 'Riki-Baka,' in the palm of his left hand—putting 'ki' in the Chinese character, and 'ka' in *kana*.[1] And she repeated many prayers for him—prayers that he might be reborn into some more happy condition.

"Now, about three months ago, in the honorable residence of Nanigashi-Sama,[2] in Kōjimachi,[3] a boy was born with characters on the palm of his left hand; and the characters were quite plain to read 'RIKI-BAKA'!

"So the people of that house knew that the birth must have happened in answer to somebody's prayer; and they caused inquiry to be made everywhere.

At last a vegetable-seller brought word to them that there used to be a simple lad, called Riki-Baka, living in the Ushigome quarter, and that he had died during the last autumn; and they sent two men-servants to look for the mother of Riki.

"Those servants found the mother of Riki, and told

her her what had happened; and she was glad exceedingly—for that Nanigashi house is a very rich and famous house. But the servants said that the family of Nanigashi-Sama were very angry about the word 'ka' on the child's hand. 'And where is your Riki buried?' the servants asked. 'He is buried in the cemetery of Zendōji,' she told them. 'Please to give us some of the clay of his grave,' they requested.

"So she went with them to the temple Zendōji, and showed them Riki's grave; and they took some of the grave-clay away with them, wrapped up in a furoshiki.[4] They gave Riki's mother some money—ten yen."[5]

"But what did they want with that clay?" I inquired.

"Well," the old man answered, "you know that it would not do to let the child grow up with that name on his hand. And there is no other means of removing characters that come in that way upon the body of a child: you must rub the skin with clay taken from the grave of the body of the former birth."

HI-MAWARI

O n the wooded hill behind the house Robert and I are looking for fairy-rings. Robert is eight years old, comely, and very wise—I am a little more than seven—and I reverence Robert. It is a glowing glorious August day; and the warm air is filled with sharp sweet scents of resin.

We do not find any fairy-rings; but we find a great many pine-cones in the high grass ... I tell Robert the old Welsh story of the man who went to sleep, unawares, inside a fairy-ring, and so disappeared for seven years, and would never eat or speak after his friends had delivered him from the enchantment.

"They eat nothing but the points of needles, you know," says Robert.

"Who?" I ask.

"Goblins," Robert answers.

This revelation leaves me dumb with astonishment and awe ... But Robert suddenly cries out:

"There is a Harper!—he is coming to the house!"

And down the hill we run to hear the harper ... But what a harper! Not like the hoary minstrels of the picture-books. A swarthy, sturdy, unkempt vagabond, with black bold eyes under scowling black brows. More like a brick-layer than a bard—and his garments are corduroy!

"Wonder if he is going to sing in Welsh?" murmurs Robert.

I feel too much disappointed to make any remarks. The harper poses his harp—a huge instrument—upon our doorstep, sets all the strong ringing with a sweep of his grimy fingers, clears his throat with a sort of angry growl, and begins, "Believe me, if all those endearing young charms, which I gaze on so fondly to-day"

The accent, the attitude, the voice, all fill me with repulsion unutterable—shock me with a new sensation of formidable vulgarity. I want to cry out loud, "You have no right to sing that song!" For I have heard it sung by the lips of the dearest and fairest being in my little world; and that this rude, coarse man should dare to sing it vexes me like a mockery—angers me like an insolence. But only for a moment! ... With the utterance of the syllables "to-day," that deep, grim voice suddenly breaks into a quivering tenderness indescribable; then, marvelously changing, it mellows into tones sonorous and rich as the bass of a great organ—while a sensation unlike anything ever felt before takes me by the throat ... What witchcraft has he learned? What secret has he found—this scowling man of the road? ... Oh! is there anybody else in the whole world who can sing like that? ... And the form of the singer flickers and dims; and the house, and the lawn, and all visible shapes of things tremble and swim before me. Yet instinctively I fear that man—I almost hate him; and I feel myself flushing with anger and shame because of his power to move me thus.

"He made you cry," Robert compassionately observes, to my further confusion—as the harper strides away, richer by a gift of sixpence taken without thanks ... "But I think he must be a gipsy. Gipsies are bad people—and they are wizards ... Let us go back to the wood."

We climb again to the pines, and there squat down upon the sun-flecked grass, and look over town and sea. But we do not play as before: the spell of the wizard is strong upon us both ... "Perhaps he is a goblin," I venture at last, "or a fairy?"

"No," says Robert—"only a gipsy. But that is nearly as bad. They steal children, you know."

"What shall we do if he comes up here?" I gasp, in sudden terror at the lonesomeness of our situation.

"Oh, he wouldn't dare," answers Robert—"not by daylight, you know."

[Only yesterday, near the village of Takata, I noticed a flower which the Japanese call by nearly the same name as we do: Himawari, "The Sunward-turning;"—and over the space of forty years there thrilled back to me the voice of that wandering harper—As the Sunflower turns on her god, when he sets, The same look that she turned when he rose.

Again I saw the sun-flecked shadows on that far Welsh hill; and Robert for a moment again stood beside me, with his girl's face and his curls of gold. We were looking for fairy-rings ... But all that existed of the real Robert must long ago have suffered a sea-change into something rich and strange ... Greater love hath no man than this, that a man lay down his life for his friend.]

HORAI

Blue vision of depth lost in height—sea and sky interblending through luminous haze. The day is of spring, and the hour morning.

Only sky and sea—one azure enormity ... In the fore, ripples are catching a silvery light, and threads of foam are swirling. But a little further off no motion is visible, nor anything save color: dim warm blue of water widening away to melt into blue of air. Horizon there is none: only distance soaring into space—infinite concavity hollowing before you, and hugely arching above you—the color deepening with the height. But far in the midway-blue there hangs a faint, faint vision of palace towers, with high roofs horned and curved like moons—some shadowing of splendor strange and old, illumined by a sunshine soft as memory.

What I have thus been trying to describe is a *kake-mono*—that is to say, a Japanese painting on silk, suspended to the wall of my alcove; and the name of it is

Shinkiro, which signifies "Mirage." But the shapes of the mirage are unmistakable. Those are the glimmering portals of Horai the blest; and those are the moony roofs of the Palace of the Dragon-King; and the fashion of them (though limned by a Japanese brush of to-day) is the fashion of things Chinese, twenty-one hundred years ago.

Thus much is told of the place in the Chinese books of that time:

In Horai there is neither death nor pain; and there is no winter. The flowers in that place never fade, and the fruits never fail; and if a man taste of those fruits even but once, he can never again feel thirst or hunger. In Horai grow the enchanted plants So-rin-shi, and Riku-go-aoi, and Ban-kon-to, which heal all manner of sickness; and there grows also the magical grass Yo-shin-shi, that quickens the dead; and the magical grass is watered by a fairy water of which a single drink confers perpetual youth. The people of Horai eat their rice out of very, very small bowls; but the rice never diminishes within those bowls—however much of it be eaten—until the eater desires no more. And the people of Horai drink their wine out of very, very small cups; but no man can empty one of those cups—however stoutly he may drink—until there comes upon him the pleasant drowsiness of intoxication.

All this and more is told in the legends of the time of the Shin dynasty. But that the people who wrote down those legends ever saw Horai, even in a mirage, is not believable. For really there are no enchanted fruits which leave the eater forever satisfied—nor any magical grass which revives the dead—nor any fountain of fairy water —nor any bowls which never lack rice—nor any cups which never lack wine. It is not true that sorrow and death never enter Horai; neither is it true that there is not any winter. The winter in Horai is cold; and winds then bite to the bone; and the heaping of snow is monstrous on the roofs of the Dragon-King.

Nevertheless there are wonderful things in Horai; and the most wonderful of all has not been mentioned by any Chinese writer. I mean the atmosphere of Horai. It is an atmosphere peculiar to the place; and, because of it, the sunshine in Horai is whiter than any other sunshine—a milky light that never dazzles—astonishingly clear, but very soft. This atmosphere is not of our human period: it is enormously old—so old that I feel afraid when I try to think how old it is; and it is not a mixture of nitrogen and oxygen. It is not made of air at all, but of ghost—the substance of quintillions of quintillions of generations of souls blended into one immense translucency—souls of people who thought in ways never resembling our ways. Whatever mortal man inhales that atmosphere, he takes into his blood the thrilling of these spirits; and they change the sense within him—reshaping his notions of Space and Time—so that he can see only as they used to see, and feel only as they used to feel, and think only as they used to think. Soft as sleep are these changes of sense; and Horai, discerned across them, might thus be described:

Because in Horai there is no knowledge of great evil, the hearts of the people never grow old. And, by reason of being always young in heart, the people of Horai smile from birth until death—except when the Gods send sorrow among them; and faces then are veiled until the sorrow goes away. All folk in Horai love and trust each other, as if all were members of a single household; and the speech of the women is like birdsong, because the hearts of them are light as the souls of birds; and the swaying of the sleeves of the maidens at play seems a flutter of wide, soft wings. In Horai nothing is hidden but grief, because there is no reason for shame; and nothing is locked away, because there could not be any theft; and by night as well as by day all doors remain unbarred, because there is no reason for fear. And because the people are fairies—though mortal—all things in Horai, except the Palace of the Dragon-King, are small and quaint and queer; and these fairy-folk do really eat their rice out of very, very small bowls, and drink their wine out of very, very small cups.

Much of this seeming would be due to the inhalation of that ghostly atmosphere—but not all. For the spell wrought by the dead is only the charm of an Ideal, the glamour of an ancient hope; and something of that hope has found fulfillment in many hearts—in the simple beauty of unselfish lives—in the sweetness of Woman.

Evil winds from the West are blowing over Horai; and the magical atmosphere, alas! is shrinking away before them. It lingers now in patches only, and bands—like those long bright bands of cloud that train across the landscapes of Japanese painters. Under these shreds of the elfish vapor you still can find Horai—but not everywhere.

Remember that Horai is also called Shinkiro, which signifies Mirage—the Vision of the Intangible. And the Vision is fading—never again to appear save in pictures and poems and dreams.

NOTES

THE STORY OF MIMI-NASHI-HŌÏCHI

1. See my *Kottō*, for a description of these curious crabs.
2. Or, Simonoséki. The town is also known by the name of Bakkan.
3. The biwa, a kind of four-stringed lute, is chiefly used in musical recitative. Formerly the professional minstrels who recited the Heiké-Monogatari, and other tragical histories, were called biwa-hoshi, or "lute-priests." The origin of this appellation is not clear; but it is possible that it may have been suggested by the fact that "lute-priests" as well as blind shampooers, had their heads shaven, like Buddhist priests. The biwa is played with a kind of plectrum, called bachi, usually made of horn.
4. A response to show that one has heard and is listening attentively.
5. A respectful term, signifying the opening of a gate. It was used by samurai when calling to the guards on duty at a lord's gate for admission.
6. Or the phrase might be rendered, "for the pity of that part is the deepest." The Japanese word for pity in the original text is *awaré*.
7. "Traveling incognito" is at least the meaning of the original phrase —"making a disguised august-journey" (*shinobi no go-ryokō*).
8. The Smaller Pragña-Pâramitâ-Hridaya-Sûtra is thus called in Japanese. Both the smaller and larger sûtras called Pragña-Pâramitâ ("Transcendent Wisdom") have been translated by the late Professor Max Müller, and can be found in volume xlix. of the Sacred Books of the East ("Buddhist Mahayana Sûtras"). Apropos of the magical use of the text, as described in this story, it is worth remarking that the subject of the sutra is the Doctrine of the Emptiness of Forms—that is to say, of the unreal character of all phenomena or noumena ... "Form is emptiness; and emptiness is form. Emptiness is not different from form; form is not different from emptiness. What is form—that is emptiness. What is emptiness—that is form ... Perception, name, concept, and knowledge, are also emptiness ... There is no eye, ear, nose, tongue, body, and mind ... But when the envelopment of consciousness has been

annihilated, then he [*the seeker*] becomes free from all fear, and beyond the reach of change, enjoying final Nirâvna."

OSHIDORI

1. From ancient time, in the Far East, these birds have been regarded as emblems of conjugal affection.
2. There is a pathetic double meaning in the third verse; for the syllables composing the proper name Akanuma ("Red Marsh") may also be read as akanu-ma, signifying "the time of our inseparable (or delightful) relation." So the poem can also be thus rendered: "When the day began to fail, I had invited him to accompany me...! Now, after the time of that happy relation, what misery for the one who must slumber alone in the shadow of the rushes!" The makomo is a short of large rush, used for making baskets.

THE STORY OF O-TEI

1. "-sama" is a polite suffix attached to personal names.
2. A Buddhist term commonly used to signify a kind of heaven.
3. The Buddhist term zokumyo ("profane name") signifies the personal name, borne during life, in contradistinction to the kaimyo ("sila-name") or homyo ("Law-name") given after death—religious posthumous appellations inscribed upon the tomb, and upon the mortuary tablet in the parish-temple. For some account of these, see my paper entitled, "The Literature of the Dead," in Exotics and Retrospectives.
4. Buddhist household shrine.
5. Direct translation of a Japanese form of address used toward young, unmarried women.

DIPLOMACY

1. The spacious house and grounds of a wealthy person is thus called.
2. A Buddhist service for the dead.

OF A MIRROR AND A BELL

1. Part of present-day Shizuoka Prefecture.
2. The two-hour period between 1 AM and 3 AM.
3. A monetary unit.

JIKININKI

1. The southern part of present-day Gifu Prefecture.
2. Literally, a man-eating goblin. The Japanese narrator gives also the Sanscrit term, "Râkshasa;" but this word is quite as vague as *jikininki*, since there are many kinds of Râkshasas. Apparently the word *jikininki* signifies here one of the *Baramon-Rasetsu-Gaki*—forming the twenty-sixth class of pretas enumerated in the old Buddhist books.
3. A *Ségaki*-service is a special Buddhist service performed on behalf of beings supposed to have entered into the condition of *gaki* (pretas), or hungry spirits. For a brief account of such a service, see my *Japanese Miscellany*.
4. Literally, "five-circle [or "five-zone"] stone." A funeral monument consisting of five parts superimposed—each of a different form—symbolizing the five mystic elements: Ether, Air, Fire, Water, Earth.

MUJINA

1. *Jinrikishas*: Literal Japanese translation is "man-powered vehicle", a *jinrikisha* is a two-wheeled cart pulled by a man. It is used as a small taxi.
2. A kind of badger. Certain animals were thought to be able to transform themselves and cause mischief for humans.
3. O-jochū ("honorable damsel"), a polite form of address used in speaking to a young lady whom one does not know.
4. An apparition with a smooth, totally featureless face, called a "nopperabo," is a stock part of the Japanese pantheon of ghosts and demons.
5. Soba is a preparation of buckwheat, somewhat resembling vermicelli.
6. An exclamation of annoyed alarm.

125

7. Well!

ROKURO-KUBI

1. The period of Eikyō lasted from 1429 to 1441.
2. The upper robe of a Buddhist priest is thus called.
3. Present-day Yamanashi Prefecture.
4. A term for itinerant priests.
5. A sort of little fireplace, contrived in the floor of a room, is thus described. The ro is usually a square shallow cavity, lined with metal and half-filled with ashes, in which charcoal is lighted.
6. Direct translation of "suzumushi," a kind of cricket with a distinctive chirp like a tiny bell, whence the name.
7. Now a rokuro-kubi is ordinarily conceived as a goblin whose neck stretches out to great lengths, but which nevertheless always remains attached to its body.
8. A Chinese collection of stories on the supernatural.
9. A present made to friends or to the household on returning from a journey is thus called. Ordinarily, of course, the *miyagé* consists of something produced in the locality to which the journey has been made: this is the point of Kwairyō's jest.
10. Present-day Nagano Prefecture.

A DEAD SECRET

1. On the present-day map, Tamba corresponds roughly to the central area of Kyōto Prefecture and part of Hyogo Prefecture.
2. The Hour of the Rat (Né-no-Koku), according to the old Japanese method of reckoning time, was the first hour. It corresponded to the time between our midnight and two o'clock in the morning; for the ancient Japanese hours were each equal to two modern hours.
3. Kaimyo, the posthumous Buddhist name, or religious name, given to the dead. Strictly speaking, the meaning of the word is sila-name. (See my paper entitled, "The Literature of the Dead" in Exotics and Retrospectives.)

YUKI-ONNA

1. An ancient province whose boundaries took in most of present-dayTōkyō, and parts of Saitama and Kanagawa prefectures.
2. That is to say, with a floor-surface of about six feet square.
3. This name, signifying "Snow," is not uncommon. On the subject of Japanese female names, see my paper in the volume entitled *Shadowings*.
4. Also spelled Edo, the former name of Tōkyō.

THE STORY OF AOYAGI

1. An ancient province corresponding to the northern part of present-day Ishikawa Prefecture.
2. An ancient province corresponding to the eastern part of present-day Fukui Prefecture.
3. The name signifies "Green Willow"—though rarely met with, it is still in use.
4. The poem may be read in two ways; several of the phrases having a double meaning. But the art of its construction would need considerable space to explain, and could scarcely interest the Western reader. The meaning which Tomotada desired to convey might be thus expressed: "While journeying to visit my mother, I met with a being lovely as a flower; and for the sake of that lovely person, I am passing the day here... Fair one, wherefore that dawn-like blush before the hour of dawn?—can it mean that you love me?"
5. Another reading is possible; but this one gives the signification of the answer intended.
6. So the Japanese story-teller would have us believe, although the verses seem commonplace in translation. I have tried to give only their general meaning: an effective literal translation would require some scholarship.

JIU-ROKU-ZAKURA

1. Present-day Ehime Prefecture.

THE DREAM OF AKINOSUKÉ

1. Present-day Nara Prefecture.
2. This name "Tokoyo" is indefinite. According to circumstances, it may signify any unknown country—or that undiscovered country from whose bourn no traveler returns—or that Fairyland of far-eastern fable, the Realm of Hōrai. The term "Kokuō" means the ruler of a country, therefore a king. The original phrase, "Tokoyo no Kokuō" might be rendered here as "the Ruler of Hōrai," or "the King of Fairyland."
3. The last phrase, according to old custom, had to be uttered by both attendants at the same time. All these ceremonial observances can still be studied on the Japanese stage.
4. This was the name given to the estrade, or dais, upon which a feudal prince or ruler sat in state. The term literally signifies "great seat."

RIKI-BAKA

1. Kana: the Japanese phonetic alphabet.
2. "So-and-so": appellation used by Hearn in place of the real name.
3. A section of Tōkyō.
4. A square piece of cotton-goods, or other woven material, used as a wrapper in which to carry small packages.
5. Ten yen is nothing now, but was a formidable sum then.

LIST OF ILLUSTRATIONS

1. Kunisada, Utagawa, *The Spectre*, (1852), Illustration, wikimedia, https://commons.wikimedia.org/wiki/File:Kunisada_The_Spectre.jpg
2. Kuniyoshi, Utagawa, *The Ghosts of Togo and His Wife*, Illustration, wikimedia, https://commons.wikimedia.org/wiki/File:Kuniyoshi_The_Ghosts_of_Togo_and_His_Wife.jpg
3. Kuniyoshi, Utagawa, *The Spirit of Sakura Sogoro Haunting Hotta Kozuke*, Illustration, uci.edu, https://faculty.humanities.uci.edu/sbklein/images/GHOSTS/maleghosts/pages/sakurasogoro03.html
4. Hashiguchi, Goyō, *Girl in a Summer Kimono*, (1920), Illustration, rawpixel, https://www.rawpixel.com/image/3813646/illustration-

image-art-people. (Source: Minneapolis Institute of Art).

5. Hashiguchi, Goyō, *Woman in Summer Clothing,* (1920), Illustration, rawpixel, https://www.rawpixel.com/image/3813853/illustration-image-art-people. (Source: Met Museum).

6. Koson, Ohara, *Blossoming Cherry on a Moonlit Night,* (ca. 1932), Illustration, raw pixel, https://www.rawpixel.com/image/2439635/free-illustration-image-japanese-art-moon. (Source: Los Angeles County Museum of Art).

7. Hokusai, Katsushika, *The Vengeful Spirits of Japan-The Midnight Society,* (1808), Illustration, picryl, https://picryl.com/media/hokusai-onryo-4fb561.

8. Gekko, Ogata, *Monk Ringing a Bell: Pictures of Japanese Flowers,* (1898), Illustration, rawpixel, https://www.rawpixel.com/image/3970485/illustration-image-flower-art-floral.

9. Kuniyoshi, Utagawa, *Kidōmaru and the Tengu,* (ca. 1840), Illustration, wikimedia, https://commons.wikimedia.org/wiki/File:Kuniyoshi_Kidomaru.jpg. (Source: Museum of Fine Arts, Boston).

10. Koson, Ohara, *Courtesan on Porch,* (1900-1910), raw pixel, Illustration, https://www.rawpixel.com/image/3045914/free-illustration-image-ohara-koson-japanese-painting. (Source: The Rijksmuseum).

11. Suushi, Sawaki, *Rokurokubi,* (ca. 1737), Illustration, wikimedia, https://commons.

wikimedia.org/wiki/
File:Suushi_Nukekubi.jpg.

12. Suushi, Sawaki, *Yūrei* (ca. 1737), Illustration, wikimedia, https://commons.wikimedia.org/wiki/File:Suushi_Yurei.jpg.

13. Shunshō, Katsukawa, *Minamoto no Yoritomo and Yuki Onna in the snow*, (1770), Illustration, wikimedia, https://commons.wikimedia.org/wiki/File:Minamoto_no_Yoritomo_en_Yuki_Onna_in_de _sneeuw.-Rijksmuseum_RP-P-2007-144.jpeg

14. Hosoda, Eishi, *Sotoori Hime,* (1756-1829), Illustration, rawpixel, https://www.rawpixel.com/image/426252/free-illustration-image-japanese-japan-woman. (Source: Library of Congress).

15. Kunisada, Utagawa, Illustration, Ukiyo-e.org, https://ukiyo-e.org/image/waseda/101-1429. (Source: Waseda University Theatre Museum).

16. Gekko, Ogata, *Woman Picking Mountain Cherry,* (1896), Illustration, rawpixel, https://www.rawpixel.com/image/3970476/illustration-image-art-people-vintage.

17. Kunisada, Utagawa, Illustration, Ukiyo-e.org, https://data.ukiyo-e.org/artelino/images/46154g1.jpg.

18. Takahashi, Hiroaki, *Junks in Inatori Bay*, (1926), Illustration, rawpixel, https://www.rawpixel.com/image/3064804/free-illustration-image-japanese-art-japan. (Source: The Los Angeles County Museum of Art).

PUBLISHER'S NOTE

This book was produced as part of the Publishing master's degree program at Western Colorado University, Graduate Program in Creative Writing. The students worked cooperatively to produce these fine new editions of worthy public-domain works. The intent is to bring literary classics to a new readership. For the enjoyment of a modern audience, some minor revisions to archaic terms or punctuation may have been made.

Because these works were written in a different time, some attitudes and phrasing may seem outdated to a modern audience. After careful consideration, rather than revising the author's work, we have chosen to preserve the original wording and intent.

ΛBOUT THE ΛUTHOR

Lafcadio Hearn was born in the Greek Ionian Islands on June 27, 1850. When he was 6 years old, he moved from the Island of Leucos to Ireland and was raised by his Irish great-aunt until the age of 16. He was then sent to the US and began working as a journalist, first in Cincinnati and then in New Orleans. He also spent time translating French literature into English and soon developed his own writing style as well as his own interests in story-telling.

In 1890, Hearn found his place in life when he traveled to Japan and became enchanted with Japanese culture, history, language, and folklore. His upbringing had been a lonely one, but he soon found his family when he fell in love with Setzu Koizumi and married her in 1891. Hearn became a Japanese citizen, took the name Yakumo Koizumi, and taught at the Imperial University for many years. He and his wife had four children, and it has been recorded that he was a loving father and family man.

Lafcadio Hearn's works demonstrate sincere love and devotion for Japan. Most entertaining are his Japanese ghost stories, which give rich insight into the history, culture, and traditions of the Japanese people. These stories were not only widely translated but also adapted into film with the movie *Kwaidan* in 1964. He remained devoted to Japan until his passing in 1904 at the age of 54.

ABOUT THE EDITOR

C. J. Anaya is a *USA Today* bestselling and award-winning author of young adult romantic fantasy and adult contemporary romance. She holds a BA in Communication from the University of Arizona Global Campus and will soon have her MA in Publishing from Western Colorado University under the tutelage of renowned *New York Times* bestselling author Kevin J. Anderson and award-winning writer and editor Allyson Longueira. Anaya has been a member of the Editorial Freelancers Association for three years and the American Night Writers Association for seven years.

For the past four years, Anaya has worked as a freelance developmental editor, specializing in romance and fantasy as well as various niches within nonfiction. She developed, and is currently teaching, an online course to help authors and entrepreneurs build their own self-publishing businesses. She works as a project manager for the same company. Anaya coaches her students in writing, book production, publishing, and marketing and has her own channel called Author Journey where authors can find free resources to assist them.

Her published works include *The Healer Series* and *Paranormal Misfits Series* (under the pen name C. J. Anaya),

Marry Your Billionaire and *Trusting the Billionaire* (under the pen name Cynthia Savage), and *Devil in Exile* (under the pen name Angelina Avery). She is currently on the editorial staff of the anthology *Gilded Glass: Twisted Myths and Shattered Fairy Tales,* executive editors Kevin J. Anderson and Allyson Longueira (Wordfire Press, July 2022).

ABOUT THE ILLUSTRATORS

Warm_Tail is the shutterstock handle for a graphic arts designer who specializes in dark fantasy. You can find this artist's work at https://linktr.ee/Warm_Tail.

Goyō Hashiguchi (1880-1921) was a leading Japanese artist in the *shin-hanga* ("new prints") movement which is considered a revival of the *ukiyo-e* style. He has fourteen woodblock prints that are considered a masterpiece within his genre.

Katushika Hokusai (1760-1849) was a Japanese artist, painter, and printer in the Edo period. He is best known for his woodblock paintings with depictions of Mount Fuji, portraiture of courtesans and couples, as well as his beautiful landscapes.

Ogata Gekko (1850-1920) was a Japanese painter and designer of woodblock prints. Having never studied at university, he was a self-taught artist, winning numerous national and international prizes.

Utagawa Kuniyoshi (1798-1861) was one of the last great masters of the ukiyo-e style and woodblock painting. He studied art at the Utagawa School. His artwork depicted aspects of Western representation, and his paintings of samurai heroes are legendary.

Sawaki Suushi was a relatively unknown artist who studied under master painter Hanabusa Itcho.

Katsukawa Shunshō (1726-1792) was a Japanese painter and printmaker. He introduced a new form of yakusha-e, which are prints that depict Kabuki actors. Although less famous, he was also praised for his bijin-ga, or prints of beautiful women.

Eishi Hosoda (1756-1829) was a Japanese painter and ukiyo-e artist. He was born into a samurai family of high rank. At that time, it was impossible to change the rank or class with which you were born. He was a samurai and painter to the upper classes.

Utagawa Kunisada (1786-1865) was a Japanese painter and designer of woodblock prints. He was also considered the most popular and prolific of his time. He worked as an apprentice under the artist Toyokuni until he was given his official artist name of Kunisada.

Hiroaki Takahashi (1871-1945) was a traditional Japanese painter. He was one of the first printmakers to join the artisan pool of Wantanabe. After the Kanto earthquake of 1923, his 500 prints were destroyed and he had to start over. He created 250 prints before he succumbed to pneumonia.

Suzuki Kason (1860-1919) was a painter known for his kuchi-e illustrations by those who collect his works. He studied traditional Japanese painting before becoming a member of the Imperial Academy of Fine Arts. Ohara Koson was one of his many students.

Ohara Koson (1877-1945) was a Japanese painter. In 1904 he began making Russ0-Japanese war prints. He also taught at the Tokyo School of Fine Arts. He was a big supporter of traditional Japanese art and woodblock painting.

Kobayashi Eitaku (1843-1890) was a Japanese artist and illustrator who specialized in the traditional woodblock painting and ukiyo-e tradition. He apprenticed under Kano Eishin. His paintings were more popular in the west as were most of his colleagues' artistic styles. His painting, *Sugawara Michizane Praying on Tenpai-zan,* won a place in The Museum of Fine Arts, Boston.

WORDFIRE CLASSICS

The Lost World
The Poison Belt
by A. Conan Doyle

The Wolf Leader
by Alexandre Dumas

The Cthulhu Stories of Robert E. Howard
by Robert E. Howard

The Detective Stories of Edgar Allan Poe
by Edgar Allan Poe

The Jewel of Seven Stars (Annotated)
by Bram Stoker

From the Earth to the Moon and Around the Moon
by Jules Verne

The Complete War of the Worlds
The War in the Air
Kipps: The Story of a Simple Man
The Sleeper Awakes and Men Like Gods
by H.G. Wells

Mother of Frankenstein: Maria: or, The Wrongs of Woman &
Memoirs of the Author of A Vindication of the Rights of
Woman
by Mary Wollstonecraft

We: The 100th Anniversary Edition
by Yevgeny Zamyatin

One Stormy Night : A Story Challenge That Created the
Gothic Horror Genre
by Lord Byron, Dr. John William Polidori, and Mary
Shelley

HOLIDAY CLASSICS
The Ghost of Christmas Always
by Charles Dickens & Kevin J. Anderson

The Santa Claus Stories
by L. Frank Baum

Our list of other WordFire Press authors and titles is
always growing. To find out more and to shop our
selection of titles, visit us at:
wordfirepress.com

 facebook.com/WordfireIncWordfirePress

 twitter.com/WordFirePress

instagram.com/WordFirePress

bookbub.com/profile/4109784512